"PLEASE—P... TURN ON THE LIGHT, MARK."

I could see the outline of Connie's body stretched out on my bed, arms thrown up over her face.

"Please!" she said. "Not the light."

I stepped into the bathroom and turned on the light there. It provided enough to see her clearly without providing any glare. I went over to the bed and sat down beside her. She turned away, moaning slightly.

"Where have you been?" I asked. "We've been crazy with anxiety for you. What's happened?"

I took hold of her hands. They were cold as ice. I pulled them gently away from her face. Suddenly she turned onto her back and looked up at me.

I say she looked up at me, but that's just a figure of speech. Her eyes were swollen and almost closed. Her whole face was dark with swellings and bruises. There was a little trickle of blood at one corner of her mouth.

She had taken a brutal beating from someone, almost beyond description.

———————— ★ ————————

HUGH PENTECOST
TIME OF TERROR

W🌐RLDWIDE.

TORONTO · NEW YORK · LONDON · PARIS
AMSTERDAM · STOCKHOLM · HAMBURG
ATHENS · MILAN · TOKYO · SYDNEY

TIME OF TERROR

A Worldwide Mystery/October 1989

First published by Dodd, Mead & Company, Inc.

ISBN 0-373-26033-4

Printed in U.S.A.

PART ONE

ONE

It BEGAN LIKE any other day. To an outsider an ordinary day at the Hotel Beaumont, New York's top luxury hotel, might have seemed thoroughly hysterical. There are hundreds of different activities that cross and recross each other like the strands in a spider's web, but to those of us in the know they all mesh together and work with the preciseness of a Swiss watch. The moment anything is slightly out of order, from the lateness of one member of the cleaning crew that takes over the lower floors in the early hours of the morning to the faint fuzziness on the telephone line into one of the thousand or more rooms a report is made and an answer found. Complaints from guests are handled quickly and efficiently; hundreds of mechanical functions from elevators, to hot water boilers, to air conditioners, down to a leaky faucet are checked and double-checked. All of this mass of minutiae is funneled into an office on the second floor, presided over by Pierre Chambrun, the legendary manager of the Beaumont. Hopefully the problems have all been solved when they reach him. If they haven't, someone is in for a tough time.

Chambrun is a short, square man with the brightest black eyes you ever saw, eyes that can be compassionate or as relentless as a hanging judge's. The hundreds of people who work for him in the Beaumont love him and respect him because they know he will always be fair and just. If you don't know how to solve a problem you go to him and ask him, but if you don't know how to solve it and you muck it up, then you are in trouble. I've sometimes thought he has a secret radar system that alerts him to troubles he couldn't possibly know about, but the truth is he knows every detail of the operation so thoroughly that so small a thing as a frown on the night bell captain's face tells him that there is something wrong. He doesn't pass it by, wondering. He inquires, and there isn't a man or woman on the staff who will hide anything from him.

The Beaumont is Chambrun's world, a city within a city. It has its own restaurants and bars and shops and hospital. It has its own maintenance crews, its sanitation crews, its security force, its press and public relations department, its accountants, its bank vaults, its lock boxes, its travel agency, its areas for banquets and balls and private business conferences, its gymnasium and sauna baths. Name it, and it exists in the Beaumont. And Chambrun, the mayor, the city manager, the king, has his finger on every item of the operation and that finger is as sensitive as a doctor's on a patient's pulse. Let there be the slightest flutter in that pulse and Chambrun is instantly on the spot, surrounded by the right people to solve the problem.

There was a day, however, when Chambrun's interlocking systems broke down a little and he was late in dealing with a problem that launched a time of terror that will not soon be forgotten.

My name is Mark Haskell, and I am the Beaumont's public relations director. I like to think that I am one of the three people in whom Chambrun places complete confidence. The others are Miss Betsy Ruysdale, his fabulous secretary, who reads his mind, anticipates his needs, protects him from a thousand minor irritations, and Jerry Dodd, head of the hotel's security force, a wiry little man with the face of a fox and the guts of a burglar, who runs the tightest ship imaginable in a world of the very rich, who are always targets for the very greedy.

My routines are different in detail every day and yet pretty much the same. It is my job to see that fashion shows, banquets, coming-out balls, conventions and other special events are given the right publicity and promotion and to see to it that no one in any department dealing with any one of these events falls short of what is required.

I have an office down the hall from Chambrun's on the second floor. I get up at eight o'clock after a normal five to six hours of sleep. I check over the schedule of events for the day. At exactly nine o'clock I report to Chambrun's office. On his desk are the registration cards from the night before and a list of guests who are expected to check in that day. Some of the guests might be a little distressed if they knew the information we had on those cards: credit ratings, is the guest an alcoholic, a woman or a man chaser, a married man double-crossing his wife, or a wife two-timing her husband, home town information of any use to us. My job is to know what guests want publicity and those who don't. A movie star from the West Coast may want a flag run up or may want complete privacy. The same goes for bank presidents or foreign diplomats. The Beaumont's proximity to the United Nations results in its being a home-away-from-home for a great many important people from other parts of the world. Local gossip columnists are on my back every day to find out who is new in the world of the

Beaumont, and it's my responsibility to leak only the
information that our guests want me to leak.

On the morning that the terror began I was in
Chambrun's office going over the guest list with him.
Chambrun's office is more like a handsome living
room than an office. The Armenian rug on the floor
is priceless. The carved Florentine desk behind which
the great man sits is a work of art. The blue-period
Picasso that looks down on him from the opposite
wall was a personal gift from the artist. There is a
richness and luxury to all the furnishings. Chambrun, following a hearty breakfast of steak or chops,
sits smoking a flat Egyptian cigarette and sipping the
foul Turkish coffee that Ruysdale brews for him on the
carved sideboard which also contains an elaborate bar.

There was nothing very touchy on the guest list that
morning and I was about to leave when Ruysdale came
in from the outer office. She looked unnaturally tense.

"There is a phone call I think you should take, Mr.
Chambrun," she said.

"Later," he said, frowning. He never takes phone
calls during this period.

"This one you must take," Ruysdale said. "And
turn on your tape recorder."

Chambrun trusted her judgment. He switched on
the tape recorder and turned on the talk box so we
could hear the conversation.

"Chambrun here," he said.

"Good morning, Mr. Chambrun," a cheerful, cultivated voice said. "In order to hold your attention, I
would like to spell out one dirty four-letter word to
you. Don't be upset. It won't embarrass the beautiful
Miss Ruysdale, whom I take it is listening. The word

is B-O-M-B—bomb. Will that hold your interest, Mr. Chambrun?"

Let me interrupt what was one of the strangest conversations I've ever heard to say that the word "bomb" turns your blood cold if you are involved in the operation of any kind of public place, like a hotel or an office or apartment building or a railroad terminal or an airport. Bombs are almost a way of life with a large segment of our society, beginning with the Irish Republican Army, the Palestinian guerrillas, and down through the various screwpot revolutionary groups that seem to operate in every country in the world. It is far from unusual to find yourself walking along a New York street and discover yourself in a crowd of people staring up at some building. When you ask, you hear the matter-of-fact words "bomb threat." A lot of these are phony alarms turned in by malicious idiots who just want to make trouble, but too many of them are not. At the Beaumont we have never had a threat, but a couple of years ago a man was torn to pieces by a letter bomb. One thing is certain. You can't ignore the threat when it comes.

Chambrun had scribbled something on a desk pad and handed it to Miss Ruysdale. "Trace this call and get Jerry."

"Who are you?" Chambrun asked in a cold, hard voice.

Miss Ruysdale hurried out into her office.

The voice on the squawk box sounded amused. "I'll save you the trouble of trying to trace this call, Chambrun. I'm calling from suite A on the fifteenth floor, normally occupied by Terrence Cleaves, the British Ambassador to the United Nations."

"Normally occupied?"

"I am occupying it at this moment, Chambrun. Shall we get back to the word bomb?"

"Who are you?" Chambrun insisted.

"Must you have a name? Well, you can call me Colonel Coriander. I am the commanding officer for the Army For Justice. We have some demands to make of you, Chambrun; demands to make of you and through you."

"So I'm listening," Chambrun said. A second light was blinking on his phone, and he signaled to me to tell Miss Ruysdale to take it in her office.

"I must try to persuade you first not to send the troops charging up here to the fifteenth floor," the voice said.

Colonel Coriander! Coriander, I thought I knew, was some kind of flower.

"Everyone on this floor has been evacuated from their rooms, Chambrun. Men who passed themselves off as members of your security force have told the guests there is a bomb threat. If someone is trying desperately to reach you on another phone, it's because your lobby is swarming with frightened people, some of them still in their pajamas and nightgowns. Know this, Chambrun. We have enough men and arms and ammunition to hold off the United States Marine Corps. They could only come down the hallway four abreast. So a head-on attack is quite futile."

"Go on. What is it you want?"

"All in good time. Some weeks ago we acquired the architect's plans for this building, Chambrun. The result is that we have placed bombs in strategic places all along this floor level. They are attached to one detonator. One false move and we blow out your elevator shafts, your fire stairs, and every room on this floor.

We will, of course, kill ourselves in the process, but it will be a little like sawing the lady in half—the lady being your hotel. Perhaps the ten stories above us will remain standing, perhaps they will go tumbling down into the street. At best they will be useless for a long, long time, and a great many people will die along with us."

"Let's assume, for the moment, that I believe you," Chambrun said.

"Oh, you'll believe me before I'm done with you," Colonel Coriander said. "Maybe no one but you will care whether your hotel is destroyed or not. So to make sure that our demands are met, we have some rather important hostages."

At that moment Jerry Dodd, our security chief, came barging into the office followed by Miss Ruysdale. Chambrun signaled for silence. Miss Ruysdale passed a pad to me to hand on to Chambrun. On it she had written: "Call coming from 15 A. Guests on that floor told there is a bomb threat. Panic in the lobby."

Colonel Coriander went on in his faintly mocking voice: "Our hostages consist of two little girls, aged ten and twelve. They are Miss Elizabeth Cleaves and Miss Mariella Cleaves, daughters of the Ambassador. There is also Miss Katherine Horn, their governess, a rather cold and unresponsive, if glamorous, chick."

"So it is a kidnapping," Chambrun said.

"Only in a semantic sense," Coriander said. "Don't you want Miss Ruysdale to pour you a fresh cup of Turkish coffee? We've got a long way to go, Chambrun."

The sonofabitch knew the details of this very private office. As if she was in a trance, Miss Ruysdale took Chambrun's cup over to the sideboard and re-filled it.

"Have you ever heard of the Army For Justice, Chambrun?"

"No."

"Well, you will after today. The whole word will after today. Let me tell you a little about us. Some of us are veterans of the war in Vietnam, some of us were war prisoners, some of us were deserters, some of us skipped the country rather than fight in an immoral war and have been denied amnesty by the men who play God. All of us are linked together by the convic-tion that it is time for justice for the people who were sold down the river by a phony peace."

"So you have a cause," Chambrun said. "I'm more interested in your demands. What is the ransom you want?"

"Don't hurry me, Chambrun. I expect to be with you for quite a while. I don't mean this conversation. I expect to be here on the fifteenth floor for days— unless you trigger us into action. It will take some time for our demands to be met."

"Get to the demands," Chambrun said. I had never heard his voice so cold and flat.

"You're going to be shocked, Chambrun, so brace yourself. There are thousands of political prisoners in South Vietnam, arrested and held by what is laugh-ingly called the democratic government there, which our government supports. Our first demand is that those prisoners be released."

"You're joking," Chambrun said.

"Far from it. Our second demand is that fifty mil-lion dollars be turned over to us to help rehabilitate those prisoners—a small amount for what they have suffered."

Jerry Dodd, his eyes wide, made a circular gesture with his finger beside his head, indicating that Coriander was a lunatic.

"Our final demand may seem rather petty to you, Chambrun," Coriander said. "There are several veterans, none above the rank of lieutenant so far as I know, who are serving jail sentences for the massacre of North Vietnamese civilians. We want them released and we want the men really responsible for the crimes placed on trial—the colonels, the generals, perhaps even the Commander-in-Chief. The men who gave the orders, who sanctioned the actions, should be punished, not the stupid pawns who carried them out."

"And if the President, the State Department, the Army, tell you to go fly a kite?" Chambrun asked.

"Then we will send these people the left ear of little Miss Elizabeth Cleaves. If they are unmoved by this, we might send them the right hand of Miss Mariella Cleaves. And so on, Chambrun, and so on. I count on your being persuasive." Coriander chuckled. "You may not be moved by an ear or a hand—or eventually a nose or a foot—but you are certain to go to great lengths to keep your own precious lady, the Beaumont, from being mutilated. And she will be, so help me God, if we come to an impasse."

"There is no chance anyone will meet these demands," Chambrun said.

"Who knows?" Coriander said. "There are millions of people in this country who are as indignant about the war in Indochina and the so-called peace as we are. Their voices may be heard when our demands

are made public. They may think that two innocent
little girls are worth more than the fascist pigs who
fake democracy, and the army pigs who pass the buck
for their own indecent and immoral outrages. Who
knows?''

"And you want me to pass on your demands?''

"With your customary eloquence.''

"Even you must know there can be no instant decisions.''

"Oh, I know. It will take time. So let me make some
things clear to you. There are thirty of us here on the
fifteenth floor. We want round-the-clock service,
meals, drinks, whatever we may fancy. We want telephone service. We know you will be listening, but shut
off the service for five minutes and you may get the
first piece of little girl flesh as a reminder.''

"Anything more?''

"Yes. I want you to believe that we have the arms,
the weapons, the bombs that we say we have. For ex-
ample, some big brain on the police force, or in the
FBI, may decide to hell with Elizabeth and Mariella
and the coldly pretty Miss Horn, and decide to tear-gas
us out. One whiff of tear gas and the man on the detonator lets go the works.''

"I believe,'' Chambrun said.

"Not good enough,'' Coriander said. "I want you
to send someone up here to see and report back to you.
To my knowledge there are just three people you
would trust. Don't send your house detective Dodd.
He might decide to be heroic and then he'd never be
able to report back. With regret, I say don't send Miss
Ruysdale. A lovely and mature woman of thirty-five—
an age at which women are at their very best—might
be too much for me to resist. I must keep my mind on

the proper priorities. So I suggest you send Mark Haskell. After all, this is a sort of public relations matter, isn't it? I'll be expecting him in the next fifteen minutes. Nice to have talked to you, Chambrun."

There was a clicking noise and silence.

TWO

IT WAS TYPICAL of Chambrun that when that incredible conversation ended he made no comment. He turned to Miss Ruysdale with a series of quick orders.

"Contact the British staff at the U.N. and have Terrence Cleaves get in touch with me at once. Try to find out where Mrs. Cleaves and the rest of the staff who live on Fifteen are."

"At once," Miss Ruysdale said, and started to leave.

"Wait, Ruysdale." He calls her Ruysdale, never Miss Ruysdale or Betsy. Some of us imagine that there is a good deal more between them than a business relationship, but nothing in his office manner to her would support such a notion. "This is not a one-order morning. I want to talk to the Police Commissioner, to the local man in charge of the FBI, to my friend James Priest in the State Department in Washington. In that order, Ruysdale."

She was gone.

Chambrun's cold eyes turned to Jerry Dodd. "Do what you can to quell the panic in the lobby, after you have taken all the self-service elevators out of action. Every elevator must have an operator. No elevator in the north wing shall go above Fourteen. The elevators in the west wing will skip Fifteen, and people located in the north wing above Fifteen will have to walk around to the west side. Alert your entire staff. Those that are off duty will report at once."

"You believe what that cockamamy jerk told you?" Jerry asked.

"I have to until I can prove he's lying. Move, Jerry."

I heard all these orders, but there was a little trickle of cold sweat running down my back. I was about to visit Colonel Coriander and his Army For Justice, and I wasn't happy about it.

"Nothing to be afraid of," Chambrun said. "He wants you to see and convince me. Most important of all, Mark, I want a detailed description of him, so detailed that a police artist can draw a perfect picture of him. Of course Coriander isn't his name. If he's telling half the truth, he has an army or draft board record. He may have a police record."

"Or a medical history out of an asylum," I said.

"One thing we know about him," Chambrun said, "is that he doesn't bother to be original."

"I thought he was about as original as anything I ever heard," I said. "Crazy original!"

"The child's ear, right out of the Getty kidnapping in Europe," Chambrun said. "Money for afflicted people and not himself, right out of the Hearst kidnapping. The release of political prisoners is from hundreds of terrorist forays here and abroad. The only fresh idea he had is to try the Pentagon generals for crimes they ordered. I had the feeling he could be talked out of that. Window dressing."

"And so?"

"And so you go up and observe as you've never observed in your life. And, Mark, if you have any chance to reassure those little girls, do what you can, even if you don't believe in it. What a God-awful thing to do to two children!"

"The whole thing is right out of a corny melo-drama," I said.

"I have the unpleasant feeling we're going to have to develop an appetite for corn," Chambrun said. "It's time for you to move, friend."

The Beaumont, as you may have guessed, is built in the shape of a large L, one arm pointing north, the other west. There are two banks of elevators, one for each wing, but if you are located in the west wing and you take the north elevators, all you have to do is walk around the L to your room.

When I left Chambrun's office, I realized I had wanted to ask him a dozen questions, all of which would have delayed my going—which was exactly what I wanted. Should I go directly to Fifteen, or should I go to Fourteen and walk up or Sixteen and walk down? If I suddenly appeared on Fifteen North, would some crazy bastard start taking shots at me? I made what I told myself was a bold decision. I would get my instructions from Colonel Coriander himself.

I walked down the flight of stairs to the lobby and found myself on the fringes of a madhouse. Dozens of people were crowded around the front desk, some of them, as Coriander had reported, in their night-clothes. Voices were high and shrill and you could smell fear.

I went over to the row of house phones near the north bank of elevators and called 15 A. The phone rang only once and then I heard Coriander's sardonic voice.

"This is Mark Haskell," I told him.

"I was beginning to wonder about you," Coriander said.

"How do I come up?" I asked.

"By elevator, unless you're on a weight reducing program and want to walk," he said.

"Is there a sentry or someone I have to get past?"

"Just walk to the door of Fifteen A and knock," Coriander said.

I decided to take the west elevators and I walked over to that bank. There were operators on each car and one of Jerry's men was standing guard. I told him that despite instructions I wanted out at Fifteen. He asked me if I didn't think that was risky.

"I've been invited by the head man," I said.

"You armed?" the man asked me.

"No."

"Want to borrow my special?"

"No chance," I said. "I'll probably be searched the first thing."

The elevator operator took me to Fifteen West. I got out, and the elevator went down, and I was alone. There wasn't a soul in sight, not a maid, not the housekeeper, not anyone. I walked slowly around the L to the north wing. No one, no guard or sentry, no sign of anyone. The entire wing was still, silent, almost as if it was deserted. I walked slowly down the corridor to the door of 15 A. I hesitated a moment. My mouth felt full of ashes.

I lifted my hand and knocked on the door. Almost before I could lower my hand, the door opened inward and I was confronted by something so unreal I had to clamp my teeth together to keep from crying out.

A man faced me, a man as tall as I am, which is just over six feet. He was unbelievable. His face was hidden by a child's Halloween mask, the kind of cardboard job you can buy in any novelty shop. It was a

pirate's face, with a black patch over one eye and a
fierce, handlebar mustache on the upper lip. On top of
that was a black fright wig, coarse hair straggling
down to his shoulders. Observe, Chambrun had said;
describe him so that a police artist can make a drawing of him. Jesus! I did observe one thing. He was
wearing a red satin dressing gown, and the left sleeve
was empty. One thing you can't disguise is a missing
arm.

"Come in, Mr. Haskell." The voice was unmistak-
able. Colonel Coriander was hiding behind all that
childish jazz.

I walked into the living room of the suite. It was a
familiar room, the furnishings Victorian. No two
suites in the Beaumont were furnished alike. The
paintings on the wall, one a Turner I knew, were
genuine, not reproductions. Only a few days ago I'd
had a chat with Terrence Cleaves in this room. There
was actually one of Cleaves's pipes resting in an ash
tray on the stretcher table behind the couch. The Ambassador was a chain pipe smoker.

"You will have to forgive my infantile makeup, Mr.
Haskell, but I'm sure Chambrun instructed you to be
able to describe me accurately for a police artist. I'm
not ready for that yet. Shall we get right down to
business?"

"What business?" I asked.

"First you are to be convinced."

After fifteen minutes I was convinced that Colonel
Coriander and his people had enough machine pis-
tols, machine guns, rifles and handguns to do just
about what he had said—hold off the United States
Marine Corps. I saw only two other men during what
Coriander called my "guided tour." Both of them

wore stocking masks over their heads. He had said thirty people, but I only saw those two. One of them was in the room which was occupied by one of Cleaves's staff next to the suite. He sat by some kind of electrified box on a table.

"One wrong move," Coriander told me, "and my friend here touches a button and—boom! Elevators, fire stairs, maybe the whole building above us comes tumbling down. And all the king's horses and all the king's men—Would you like to see where the explosives are planted?"

I was shown whether I wanted to see or not. Sticks of dynamite, or some other substance, wrapped together, wired to each other. They were located in every room I was shown, along the hall, in the service area, the linen closets, outside the elevator shaft and, I was assured, inside the shaft, too. There were crates and crates of ammunition for the guns. How this had all gotten in here, I couldn't guess.

When we finally got back to the sitting room in 15 A, my undershirt and shirt were wet with sweat, sticking to me.

"Satisfied?" Coriander asked.

"Satisfied," I said.

"I wanted to be sure that Chambrun didn't assume I was overstating my case."

"I'll make certain he knows that," I said.

"What has he done so far?"

"He's trying to contact the Cleaves family and staff, to begin with."

"He should have asked me. I could have told him where they were," Coriander said. "The Ambassador is at the United Nations, along with the three male members of his staff and his two female secretaries.

Mrs. Cleaves has gone shopping—Saks Fifth Avenue, she said. I suspect she'll be coming back pretty soon."

"You plan to hold her, too?"

"Dear me, no," Coriander said. "You see, we chose just the right moment to take over, Haskell. There was no one in this suite or the rooms occupied by the Ambassador's staff except the two little girls and the governess. We just moved in with them. No need for violence."

"They can be frightened to death without violence," I said.

"Very brave little girls," Coriander said. "I do hope it won't be necessary to harm them. That, of course, is up to all the people I suspect Mr. Chambrun is already contacting—the police, the FBI, the State Department, the Pentagon. I wouldn't put it past your extraordinary boss to be talking to the President of the United States at this very moment."

"If he thought it was necessary," I said.

"He better begin to think so," Coriander said.

You might think there would have been an impulse to laugh at this man in his kid's disguise. There wasn't. Behind that mocking, amused voice was a toughness that left nothing at all to laugh at.

"I know that Terrence Cleaves is very well off financially," Coriander said. "But I don't expect him to be able to raise fifty million dollars from his own sources."

"Who do you expect will pay you?" I asked.

All traces of humor disappeared from his voice, and it rose slightly with a kind of intense anger. "The United States of America," he said. "The men who bombed and massacred innocent civilians, the men who support a government that imprisons thousands of dissenters in tiger cages, the men who defoliated and destroyed a nation's crops so that little children starved to death, their bellies swollen, the men who gave the orders that resulted in the mutilation of thousands of men like me!'' He was suddenly clutching his empty sleeve with his right hand, and his knuckles were white.

''Are there instructions for delivering the money?'' I asked.

He seemed to let his breath out in a long sigh, and the crazy pirate's mustache quivered. ''There will be time enough for instructions,'' he said. ''The money is to be used to help rehabilitate the men and women in those tiger cages in Indochina. Until they are released, there is no use for the money. In case Chambrun does get to talk to the President, he might warn him that if there is too much delay I might send him a little girl's ear on toast for his lunch break in the Oval Office.''

I had the feeling he wasn't kidding.

''How do we know the Cleaves children are still in one piece?'' I asked him.

''The last part of your tour,'' he said. ''Come with me.''

The suite consists of the living room we were in, and down a short corridor were two bedrooms and two baths. Coriander took me to one of the bedrooms and there were the two little girls and their governess. I had seen the children in the lobby of the hotel, beautifully turned out, almost ethereal in their looks. One of them was golden blonde and the other reddish. They wore their hair well down below their shoulders. Nice bones, wide friendly mouths, and eyes which, when they looked at me, were dark with fear.

Coriander, despite his comic mask, adopted a manner of almost formal courtesy. "Mr. Haskell, may I introduce you to Miss Elizabeth Cleaves and Miss Mariella Cleaves."

The little girls' mouths moved, but I didn't hear any sound. Then the undertones of laughter came back into Coriander's voice. "And this gorgeous dark lady of the sonnets is Miss Katherine Horn, who bears the unglamorous official title of governess."

Katherine Horn was something to look at, dark hair and eyes and a luscious mouth and figure. She stood, very erect, between the girls, an arm around each of them. She was staring intently at me.

"Mr. Haskell is a messenger boy from the powers-that-be," Coriander said. "If you want to send some kind of word to your parents, girls, I'm sure he'll be glad to carry it for you. And you, Miss Horn, if there is some pining boyfriend who craves your flesh, word might be gotten to him, too."

"Can you help us?" Katherine Horn asked me in a low, husky voice.

"I'll do my best," I said.

Without looking at Coriander, she said: "This man is quite mad, you know. No one on earth will meet his demands."

"Things are in motion to see what can be done," I said.

"God help us," Katherine Horn said.

"Is there something I can tell your mother and father, girls?" I asked.

"That we love them," Elizabeth said, in a small voice.

"That we're all right, not hurt," Mariella said, in a stronger voice. She was the redhead.

"That we'll try to be brave," Elizabeth said.

"That we're not afraid," Mariella said.

"That it would be nice to see them."

"That we're sure they're doing whatever is necessary to have us released."

"I'll pass all that along to them," I said.

"Thank you, sir," they said, together.

Coriander took me back to the living room. I felt even more shaken than I had been before I saw the girls and Miss Horn.

"Miss Horn creates something of a problem," Coriander said, laughter behind the words again. "There are more than twenty of us up here who have not taken the monastic vows of celibacy. It would be so much easier if she would opt for pleasure instead of heroism." He shook his head as though it was beyond him. "So, you have seen our fortress, Mr. Haskell, and you have seen the little lovelies who are our leverage. I think you can assure Mr. Chambrun that we can hold off any kind of attack, and that if we are driven to it, we can blow his hotel to hell and gone."

"I'll tell him what I've seen," I said. I wanted to get out of there. I had come up to 15 A a little scared, but certain that we were being confronted by some kind of massive bluff. I was convinced now that Coriander wasn't bluffing, and that he was, as Katherine Horn had said, quite mad, quite capable of carrying out any threats he made.

"There are one or two small points I would like to pass on to Chambrun," Coriander said. "I have explained to him that we must have room service at all times. Just in case anyone got the wild idea that we could be poisoned by what we eat or drink, let them know that the little girls will taste everything first. It

will be necessary for some of us to come and go from
time to time. We are not to be interfered with. If any
one of my people is stopped, questioned, held, you
will instantly receive evidence that one of the girls has
paid a price for it. Clear?"

"Quite clear," I said.

He laughed. "I wonder how you will describe me to
Chambrun."

I tried not to look at his empty sleeve. "You've
made that impossible," I said.

"Perhaps we'll meet again," he said. "I shall insist
on your being my contact with Chambrun. Good-bye,
Haskell. Be persuasive."

And then I was out in the hall and literally running
toward the west wing.

I SUPPOSE different people react in different ways to
moments of high tension. I find myself suddenly aware
of absurd details, enlarged and magnified. Standing
outside the elevator door on 15 West I noticed that a
tiny piece of the brass number on the door had been
chipped away; down the hall the door to the linen
room stood open, a violation of the rules. Then I remembered that everyone had been ordered off the
floor by Coriander, probably in panic. Then I remembered the elevator wasn't going to stop at 15 no
matter how long I rang the bell. Chambrun's orders.

I ran for the fire stairs, breathing as hard as if I'd
covered an Olympic mile. I'd only gone a few steps
down when I was confronted by two of Jerry Dodd's
men. They had instructions to check on anyone who
came to or left the fifteenth floor, but to let them go.
Of course they knew me. How bad was it up there?
What about the little girls? I told them the danger was

very real and that, so far, the girls and Miss Horn were still in one piece. I thought of Coriander threatening to send the President of the United States something for his lunch break in the Oval Office. Tomato surprise! You lift the cover and there is a little girl's ear. Jesus!

An elevator stopped for me at 14. I was instantly conscious of a wart on the back of the operator's neck. I wondered if the poor son of a bitch knew he might be dying of cancer.

I was let out at the second floor and into bedlam. The corridor, all the way from the elevator to Chambrun's office, was jammed with people, all talking and some shouting at once. Most of them were hotel guests. There was a sprinkling of reporters I recognized, and they set up a roadblock for me. Was it true I'd been up to 15? Was there any real danger? Evidently nothing had leaked yet about Coriander or his hostages, because nobody asked me about them. It wouldn't be long before the whole story broke, and then God help us all.

I edged my way through protesting people to the door of Chambrun's office. Two more of Jerry's men were holding back the crowd. They let me through into Miss Ruysdale's outer sanctum. Miss Ruysdale's telephones were being manned by a girl from the business office, which meant that Miss Ruysdale was inside with the boss. I went through into Chambrun's office, where I found him surrounded by people, most of them strangers to me except, of course, Miss Ruysdale, and the handsome, copper-haired woman I knew to be Constance Cleaves, the mother of the two little girls I'd just left upstairs.

Animated conversation ended abruptly and everyone in the room was focused on me. I looked at
Chambrun for instructions, but his blank stare told me
nothing. Constance Cleaves came at me, almost running across the thick rug.

I had seen this woman around the hotel but we'd
never had any conversations together. She was strik-
ingly beautiful, with high cheekbones, wide mouth,
and dark blue eyes set off by that coppery hair. She
must have married Cleaves and had her children when
she was very young, for I took her to be not much
more than thirty. The Ambassador had to be in his
early fifties. She had a gorgeous figure set off by
clothes that had been designed for her by a genius. She
had gone shopping that morning in a simple cotton
print that I knew, from my contacts with fashion
shows, had set the Cleaves exchequer back about four
hundred bucks.

Her low, husky voice shook me, because she was
obviously fighting terror. "You saw the girls, Mr.
Haskell?"

I tried to sound reassuring. "I saw them. They're
fine, Mrs. Cleaves. They said to tell you that they're
fine, that they aren't afraid."

"Thank God!" she said.

"They said to tell you they know you're doing
everything you can to get them released."

She turned away from me and her voice rose in a
sort of cry of despair. "What are we doing? What in
God's name are we doing?"

No one answered her. She turned back to me.

"I don't think you need to worry for the time being,
Mrs. Cleaves," I said. "They don't expect decisions to
be made quickly. The girls are being kept in one of the

bedrooms with Miss Horn, who appears to have kept her cool.''

Rather astonishingly, Constance Cleaves laughed—a short, sharp little laugh. ''Katherine can be depended on to be cool,'' she said. No love lost there, I thought. I remember thinking that while her speech pattern was cultivated, it didn't sound British. I wondered if Terrence Cleaves had married an American.

''I think you can count on the girls' being safe for the time being, Mrs. Cleaves,'' Chambrun said in a hard, flat voice. ''If you will forgive us, there are a great many questions we need to ask Mark.''

Several of the strange men in the room started to ask questions at the same time, but Chambrun cut them off.

''First, a description of Coriander, Mark,'' he said.

''No dice,'' I said. ''Would you believe he was wearing a kid's Halloween mask and a wig? I saw two other men, both wearing stocking masks. There is one thing, though. Coriander's left arm is missing.''

''That narrows it down some,'' one of the men said. ''An amputee, served in Vietnam. Hospital records.''

This man was a slim, dark, thoughtful-looking fellow who turned out to be the local head of the FBI, Augustus V. Brand, known as Gus to his intimates. I came to like and respect him in the time ahead, but at that moment he was a zero to me. He spoke to a young man standing next to him who took off, apparently to check on Vietnam amputees. I told myself that could be a life work.

Two men who had ''cop'' written all over them were standing to the left of Chambrun's desk. One, a bald, sharp-eyed man with a fringe of blond hair around his shiny skull, was the Assistant Commissioner of Police named Treadway. The other was a great hulk of a man with a shock of iron-gray hair and unpleasant narrowed eyes. He turned out to be Captain Valentine of the bomb squad. Chambrun introduced them both.

"These gentlemen are interested in what else you saw, Mark," he said.

"Just as Coriander said on the phone, enough guns and ammunition to hold off an army."

"What kind of guns?" the Assistant Commissioner asked.

"Machine pistols, rifles, handguns. Boxes and trunks full of ammunition."

"How did they get all that stuff up there without anyone noticing?" Treadway asked Chambrun.

Chambrun just shook his head.

"Explosives?" Captain Valentine asked.

"In every room I was shown; perhaps twelve of the twenty rooms in the north wing. Outside the elevator shaft and I was assured inside the shaft, too."

"But you didn't see inside the shaft?"

"No."

"How did you come down, Mark?" Chambrun asked. "From Fourteen or Sixteen?"

"Fourteen," I said. "I went down the fire stairs from Fifteen."

"Did you see any explosives on the fire stairs?"

"No, but I have to tell you I wasn't looking. I was in a hell of a hurry to get out of there. Two of Jerry's men were on the stairs, though. They could tell you."

"What kind of explosives?" Valentine, the bomb squad man, asked.

"I'm no expert," I said. "It looked like sticks of dynamite tied together in little bundles. Each one has a wire running from it to the next one. In the room next to Fifteen A one of those stocking-masked creeps is sitting in front of some kind of electric control box. One wrong move, Coriander told me, and he presses the button that blows up the works."

"Could they set off a whole string of charges like that at one time?" the Assistant Commissioner asked Valentine.

"Sure they could. And if some jerk tries cutting one of those connecting wires, he could set it off for them," Valentine said.

"Of course you're going to have to evacuate the hotel, Mr. Chambrun," Treadway said.

"I think not," Chambrun said. He sat hunched in his desk chair, looking like an inscrutable Buddha, a curl of smoke from one of his Egyptian cigarettes forcing him to narrow his bright, black eyes. "Not just yet—"

"But, my God, man!" Valentine said. "They're set to blow your hotel into the East River."

"They won't commit suicide until all the negotiations have failed, and that can take a long time," Chambrun said.

"Or until someone makes a wrong move," I said.

"What kind of wrong move?" Treadway asked.

"How the hell do I know?" I said. "Anything that displeases Coriander."

"Anything that threatens him," Chambrun said. "We're dealing with a zealot with a cause."

"You're just going to let people stay in the rooms without telling them they're sitting on a volcano?" Gus Brand, the FBI man, asked. "I mean the word's out, isn't it?"

Chambrun's lips moved in a tight little smile. "Everyone will be warned and I'll make you a bet, Mr. Brand. Not ten people will leave the hotel until they are ordered out."

"Which will be when?" Brand said.

"When I think the danger is acute," Chambrun said.

"The Commissioner may not go for that," the Assistant Commissioner said.

"And the danger won't be acute until they have first mutilated my children and Katherine Horn," Constance Cleaves said in a shaken voice.

That brought us all back to something besides bricks and mortar and steel girders. The hostages would be used to keep us in line before Coriander admitted defeat and blew up Chambrun's world.

The little red button on Chambrun's desk phone blinked, and Miss Ruysdale, who was standing right by the desk, picked it up and answered. She looked at Chambrun, her face expressionless.

"An order for luncheon for thirty people on the fifteenth floor," she said.

"It's to be filled, of course," Chambrun said. "Served to them however they want it served."

"How about a couple of our men to act as waiters?" the Assistant Commissioner suggested.

"Not worth the risk just yet," Chambrun said. "Coriander knows this hotel too well. He suggested on the phone that Ruysdale serve me a cup of Turkish coffee. Only someone who's been in this office knows about that Turkish coffee maker. He's smuggled in guns and arms and ammunition without being detected. That means he knows our routines inside out. It would surprise me if he didn't have a rundown on every bellhop and waiter in the place, everyone on Jerry Dodd's security force. Right now I think it would be a mistake to play it any way but absolutely straight with him."

"So we just let him have his way?" Treadway said, a muscle rippling along the line of his jaw.

"Until the people who must meet his demands—if they are to be met—have evaluated the situation. It gives us time to plan some kind of move in case the answers are all 'no.'"

"What kind of move?" Gus Brand asked.

"The one right one," Chambrun said. "Because, gentlemen, we'll never get a second chance."

Just then the party enlarged as Terrence Cleaves, the Ambassador, and the man I knew to be his executive assistant came charging into the office. An astonishing thing happened. Cleaves didn't go to his wife to comfort her. He walked straight past her as though she weren't there and confronted Chambrun.

"How bad is it?" he asked.

THREE

TERRENCE CLEAVES was a striking-looking man. He stood over six feet tall with a trim, athletic body to match. He had been something of a sports figure in his younger days, an international cricket star, a six-goal polo player, had once reached the semifinals in the British Amateur Golf Championship. His face was that of a typical British aristocrat: high cheekbones, broad forehead, a little military mustache over a straight, firm mouth, with deep crow's-feet at the corners of bright black eyes. His hair was curly, modern-styled, gray at the temples. A man of distinction. Like most of Britain's wealthy upper class, money inherited from his father and his father's father, he had gone into government as a career. He had served in at least two cabinets after World War II, in which he had been decorated for bravery. He was now Ambassador to the United Nations.

Perhaps anxiety for his children, justified God knows, had made him brush past his wife as he had, but I wondered. I looked at her and her lovely face was twisted into a little mask of pain.

Douglas Horween, who came in with Cleaves, was, I knew, given the title of executive assistant to the ambassador. He was eye-catching in his own right. About forty, I imagined, with brick-red hair, mod-styled, long but in perfect order. He was about my height, a little shorter than Cleaves. He had a pug nose, a square jaw, and a face with laughing lines at the corners of his mouth and eyes. But there was no laughter in his eyes, pale blue and as cold as newly minted dimes. He was wearing a seersucker jacket and beautifully cut gray slacks. His shoes were custom-made. A man of expensive tastes, as suggested by the pale blue silk shirt and the dark blue club tie. We have pretty complete files on most of our guests at the Beaumont, and Douglas Horween's card indicated that he had been a British Intelligence agent until he joined Cleaves's staff about three years ago. He had been an expert on China and most of the other Far Eastern countries. Rumor had it that he'd been dropped from the Service after too much publicity had been given to the assassination of some Cambodian big shots. He was a tough, tough cookie from all accounts.

It was Horween who stopped by Constance Cleaves. It was Horween who put his hand gently on her shoulder. I heard him speak to her in his very British voice.

"Chin up, love," he said. "We'll get them back. I promise you."

I thought she flinched a little under his touch, but she looked up at him with her fear-darkened eyes. "How?" she asked him.

Horween moved past her to stand next to Cleaves, facing Chambrun. Treadway, the Assistant Commissioner, Valentine, the bomb man, and Gus Brand, the FBI man, moved away into a little huddle while Chambrun outlined Coriander's demands again to the Ambassador. Cleaves stood as straight and still as a Coldstream Guardsman outside Buckingham Palace. Horween fidgeted with a pack of cigarettes—English Players—but never got to light one.

When Chambrun had finished, Terrence Cleaves spoke in a hollow-sounding voice. "Two hundred and fifty million is an astronomical amount," he said, "but I suppose there might be some way to raise it. But the rest—"

"The United States would have to send its bloody army back to Vietnam to release those prisoners," Horween said. "The South Vietnamese would never do it voluntarily. Their own lives are worth more to them than Elizabeth's, or Mariella's, or Katherine's. Released, those prisoners would throw the present South Vietnamese government down the nearest sewer." He turned to me, and I thought those pale cold eyes might be reading the shirtmaker's label on the inside of my collar. "You've been over the fifteenth floor, Haskell?"

I gave him a quick rundown.

"There is no such thing as an impenetrable fortress," he said when I'd finished. "There has to be a way to get to the girls and get them out."

"You have a notion?" Chambrun asked. He hated bravado, and it sounded in his voice.

"Getting in and out of places has been my life's work," Horween said. "What about food—room service?"

"A luncheon order for thirty is being prepared for them now," Chambrun said.

"Served by?"

"Regular staff."

"So I become a member of the regular staff," Horween said.

Chambrun explained, patiently, his conviction that Coriander knew the workings of the hotel and its staff.

Bring in an outsider and Coriander might decide we were not showing good faith.

Horween gave the great man a tight, frozen smile. "One of my better skills lies in the art of disguise," he said. "If there is a waiter in your room service group who is at least six feet tall and who can be assigned to deliver this first order, let me see him, study him. I promise you that by suppertime I can take his place and I promise you your one-armed monster will never on this earth detect the substitution."

"It's too risky, Douglas," Cleaves said. "One mistake and Elizabeth and Mariella will pay for it."

"And Katherine," Horween said. "You know my history, Terrence. I don't make mistakes."

The law had come back to join the circle and it was Gus Brand, the FBI man, who added his objections to Horween's idea. "I don't think we can risk any one-man heroics at this time," he said.

Horween looked at him as though he wasn't very bright. "It may come to that sooner or later," he said. "You can't afford not to prepare for it now. Let me look over the room service crew for a waiter whose place I can take later. You can all be the jury that decides whether I can pass for him when the time comes." He turned to Cleaves. "Don't overlook the chance for something later, Terrence. You may regret it all the rest of your life." He looked now at Constance Cleaves, but he didn't speak to her.

"Please, Terrence," she said to her husband.

"It's really up to the people in charge," Cleaves said, still turned away from her. He seemed to want something from Chambrun who, in turn, was studying Horween.

"I see no harm in letting Mr. Horween show us what he can do," he said. "Provided it's understood he makes no move without our consent."

"Understood," Horween said. "But let me pick out a waiter now, quickly. When I take his place, you'll have a much more detailed report than Haskell is able to give us." He smiled at me. "No offense, old man, but checking out a place like that is my profession."

I hadn't a doubt he might see things I'd overlooked.

Gus Brand exchanged glances with the bomb squad man and the Assistant Commissioner. He shrugged. "I'm willing to look at what you can do, Horween," he said. "If we could get a man on the inside it would be a big help."

"So let's stop stalling," Horween said.

I thought I might get the assignment of taking Horween down to the room service depot, but Chambrun had something else in mind for me, and it was Miss Ruysdale, with detailed instructions, who went off with our would-be hero.

Still there was nothing between the Cleaveses. The Ambassador had no word for his wife, no gesture of sympathy or reassurance. They were hostile strangers. When Horween had left the office, Constance Cleaves walked over to the far windows and stood with her back to us, looking down at the park. I remembered that the two girls, Elizabeth and Mariella, had gone to the park to play almost every morning under the protection of Katherine Horn. Constance was looking for ghosts, I thought.

"Reporters are going to break down these office doors if we don't have a statement for them soon,"

Chambrun said. "The question, gentlemen, is what kind of statement?"

"No kind of silence has been imposed on us, from what you've told me," Treadway, the Assistant Commissioner, said. "Coriander started the bomb scare himself by getting all your guests off the fifteenth floor. If room service people are going to be in and out, the presence of the Cleaves children and Miss Horn will leak. I don't know that any limits have been imposed on us. It may be quite refreshing to be able to tell the whole truth about something with political overtones."

"Oh, I think Coriander wants the whole truth told," Chambrun said. "He thinks millions of people may sympathize with his cause when it's made public."

"If this Army For Justice really exists, there must be other members of it outside the hotel," Gus Brand, the FBI man, said. "I think what is released to the press and the media may not be in our hands at all." I kept thinking he looked more like a college professor than a top manhunter. "Our major concern, it seems to me, has to be the safety of the Cleaves children and Miss Horn. What you, personally, release to the press, Mr. Chambrun, should be guided by that."

"In what way?" Terrence Cleaves asked. He sounded like a man who had been drained of all emotion—flat, cold, defeated in some way.

"The most important thing is to keep all the crackpots, souvenir hunters, crazy people, away from the fifteenth floor," Brand said. "It's my opinion that the best course is to tell the press that the Cleaves children and their governess have been kidnapped, are being held in Fifteen A, and that a ransom has been demanded. There is the threat of a bombing if anyone tries to interfere. Mr. Cleaves is in the process of trying to meet the kidnappers' demands. He needs time and elbow room. People will keep their hands off, one hopes, if they know they might be responsible for harming the children.''

"Oh, God!'' It was a whisper from the woman standing by the windows.

Chambrun put out his cigarette in the brass ash tray on his desk. There was something emphatic about it, as though he'd made up his mind about the whole problem.

"One of the reasons I don't think much of Horween's scheme, no matter how skillful he is at disguise, is that we are living in a goldfish bowl as far as Coriander is concerned. You're right, Mr. Brand, about one thing. We have to assume that not all the Army For Justice is holed up on the fifteenth floor. Some of them may be guests in the hotel. Some of them may actually be working in the kitchen or on the room service staff.''

"You don't trust your people?'' Cleaves asked.

"I trust them to function efficiently and not to steal from me,'' Chambrun said. "I can't trust them not to espouse causes with which I have no sympathy. It goes deeper than that, however. Coriander or someone close to him knows the routines of this office, as I explained.'' He waved at the Turkish coffee maker on the sideboard. "So they can be all around us. Some wide-eyed reporter asking us questions may actually be a member of the army, acting as ears for Coriander. As I said, we are in a goldfish bowl. We have to assume, for the moment, that any move we make will be known to Coriander almost before we make it. That's why I'm not keen for Horween's notion. While he's disguising himself to look like one of our waiters, that waiter himself may be a member of Coriander's army."

"Aren't you overreacting?" Treadway, the Assistant Commissioner, asked.

"Perhaps," Chambrun said, "but that may be the best way to keep the Cleaves children in one piece."

Valentine, the big, gray bomb squad cop, stirred restlessly. "Talk isn't getting me anyplace," he said. "The press is your problem, not mine. I need to find out exactly what kind of explosives are being used. I need to talk to the architect and the builder of the Beaumont, if they're still available. I need blueprints of the building. We have to know just how much damage a big blow will do. You may have to evacuate floors above and below Fifteen, Chambrun. Anything new, let me know."

We watched him lumber out of the office. At least he was doing something, which was more than I could say for the rest of us.

"You really think there's anything to Coriander's notion that there'll be a lot of people sympathizing with his aims when the story breaks?" Treadway asked.

"This country was split down the middle over Vietnam," Gus Brand said. "The people who were opposed to the war made a hell of a lot more noise than the people who were for it. So even if it wasn't an even split, it sounded like it. Split over Vietnam, over Watergate, over impeachment, over the economy. Properly sold, Coriander could have millions of very vocal supporters."

"But nobody will meet his demands," Treadway said. "Horween was right, you know. They'd have to start a new war to get those prisoners free. And can you imagine the Pentagon sending their generals to jail?"

"There is the money," Gus Brand said quietly. His soft brown eyes were fixed on Terrence Cleaves. Constance Cleaves turned from the windows, waiting for her husband to speak. He was still the immovable, stone-faced Coldstream Guardsman, looking at a spot on the wall just above and beyond Chambrun's head—a blank spot on the wall.

"In most people's terms I am a rich man," he said finally. "I suppose I am worth, approximately, five million pounds." I did some quick arithmetic and figured he was talking about ten to twelve million dollars. Only a small part of what Coriander was demanding.

"Friends who will help?" Brand asked.

A nerve twitched high up on Cleaves's cheek. "A hundred million pounds?" He shook his head slowly from side to side.

"You damn well better appear to be trying," Chambrun said sharply. "We have to appear to be trying to meet at least one of Coriander's demands to have any basis for negotiating with him. What would your first move be?"

"I haven't the faintest notion," Cleaves said so softly it was almost inaudible.

"You go, openly, to your banking affiliations here in New York," Chambrun said. He sounded impatient. "You meet, publicly, with the British Ambassador in Washington. You talk to our State Department man when he gets here."

"Do you really think governments are going to help me raise the money?" Cleaves asked.

"Who knows?" Chambrun said. "People will recognize that they can't free the prisoners and that they won't try their generals." He glanced at Constance. "I have to be brutal, just this once, Mrs. Cleaves. Money is something the people know governments have. If money will keep the hostages from being mutilated, a great many people will think governments ought to get it up. You have to make a try for it, Cleaves—now, quickly. If you care."

That jolted Cleaves back into reality. "Just what the bloody hell do you mean—if I care?" He still didn't look at his wife. For some mysterious reason they weren't sharing this tragedy.

"I mean, get off your butt—if you understand what that particular piece of American slang means," Chambrun said.

A PRIVATE DINING ROOM on the main floor, opening off the Grand Ballroom, was designated as a place where Chambrun and I would take on the press and the media. The Assistant Commissioner had departed to talk things over with his immediate boss and the mayor. Gus Brand, the FBI man, was marshaling his forces, I assumed, and trying to run down and identify a Vietnam veteran who had lost his left arm in the service who might now be Colonel Coriander. Somewhere a computer should turn up any previous information that had been collected on the Army For Justice.

There was a mass of detail to be organized in this emergency, but one of the best ways to be free to act was to get rid of the press, get them out of our hair.

There was a little raised platform at one end of the private dining room. The speakers' table. Chambrun and I approached it from the kitchen and found ourselves confronted by wall-to-wall faces. We hadn't, of course, been listening to radio or television in the last hour and we discovered the minute we stepped into the room that Coriander had beaten us to the draw. The whole story was out: the hostages, the specifics of the demands, the threat to the Cleaves children and Katherine Horn, and the danger to the hotel and its guests.

Everybody in the room shouted questions to us at the same time. Chambrun held up his hands for quiet and then said, "One at a time, please." Of course they all began shouting in concert again.

"Apparently we haven't anything very new to tell you," Chambrun said, when he had quieted them again. The Cleaves girls and their governess were prisoners in 15 A. I had been up there and seen the arms, ammunition, and explosives.

A young man in the very front row whom I didn't know raised his hand to be recognized and the crowd seemed to realize that was the only way it was going to work.

"Colin Andrews of the *London Times*," the young man said, identifying himself. He was a rather intense, pleasant-looking fellow with wire-rimmed glasses that were slightly tinted. His hands were jammed in the pockets of his pale gray tropical worsted suit. He wasn't taking notes.

"You talked with this Colonel Coriander?" he asked me.

"Yes."

"So you can describe him."

"No." I explained why, and a rumble of voices started around the room again.

"He gave you his demands?"

"He'd already made them to Mr. Chambrun over the phone. I was sent up to make sure he wasn't bluffing."

"And you're convinced he isn't?"

"The Cleaves children and Miss Horn are there; the guns and ammunition are there; the explosives are there and set in place. I was convinced."

"What is being done about it?" This question was aimed at Chambrun.

"The police have been notified and the bomb squad is on the premises," Chambrun said. "The FBI, the State Department, and the Pentagon are aware of what's going on."

"And what is the hotel doing, Mr. Chambrun?"

"The fifteenth floor has been evacuated—left to these people. If the bomb squad advises it, we may evacuate a floor or two above and below Fifteen in the north wing. Otherwise we will function as usual."

"My God!" someone said.

Young Mr. Andrews was persistent. "How are the Cleaveses taking it?" he asked.

"How would you expect them to take it?" Chambrun said. "They're in shock, but they are just as brave as the little girls are."

"Can Cleaves raise the money?" Andrews asked.

"Naturally that's his first concern," Chambrun said.

"But can he raise it?"

"I have no way of answering that question, Mr. Andrews. But Ambassador Cleaves is a man of influence, with many friends who can be counted on to help him in every way possible."

A strange thing happened. Andrews laughed, a short, bitter little laugh. "Name three!" he said, turned around and began working his way toward the rear of the room.

I don't remember much about that press conference after that. It was pretty chaotic, with the same questions being asked over and over until Chambrun finally called a halt.

"There is too much to be done for us to go on with this," he said. "Mark Haskell will have a statement for you at nine o'clock each morning and five o'clock each afternoon, unless something breaks in between times."

An astonished reporter asked: "You expect this to go on for days, Mr. Chambrun?"

"I expect there will be proposals and counterproposals," Chambrun said. "Coriander expects it to take time. As long as the negotiations appear to be in good faith, I expect it to take time. We are going to be dealing with governments and government agencies, none of which move quickly."

"Do you seriously believe Coriander's demands will be considered?"

"It's too soon for me to make an educated guess," Chambrun said. "And now, ladies and gentlemen, that will be all for now."

CHAMBRUN AND I took off through the ballroom kitchens and walked up the fire stairs to the second floor. Jerry Dodd's men had pretty well cleaned out the second floor corridor and we had no trouble bypassing the handful of hotel guests who were eager to talk to the boss. He kept moving, mumbling apologies to these people, some of them old-timers who had lived at the Beaumont for years. Almost all of them were people who had been evacuated from the fifteenth floor. They had no place to go, their belongings were, in effect, in Coriander's hands. Chambrun promised them, as he moved along, that arrangements would be made to take care of them in a very few minutes.

At last we were in Miss Ruysdale's office with the door to the outside world closed behind us. The handsome Ruysdale was standing with her back to the door of Chambrun's office.

"Mrs. Cleaves is still inside," she told us. "I thought she needed time to get pulled together."

"Quite right," Chambrun said. "The Ambassador?"

"Gone to borrow a few million dollars from somewhere," Ruysdale said.

Chambrun hesitated, looking past his secretary at the closed door. "Is there gossip about the Cleaveses' marriage?" he asked.

"Nothing I could find on a quick check," Ruysdale said. She was always ahead of the game. She'd known Chambrun would ask. "Mr. Priest of the State Department arrives at Kennedy in about a half hour," she went on. She was checking her notebook. "He should be here by one o'clock. The word from Washington is do nothing till you've talked to him."

"Did they expect me to free the Vietnam prisoners?" Chambrun asked. I recognized his mood. He was bitter about the disruption of his precious hotel. I don't mean to say he wasn't concerned about the Cleaves children, but the two things were closely interlocked. "Get Jerry Dodd back up here when he can come," he said. "Come with me, Mark."

We went into his office. Constance Cleaves was sitting in one of the deep, green leather armchairs, her head resting back against it, her eyes closed. The minute she heard us, she uncoiled like a spring and was on her feet.

"Nothing new, Mrs. Cleaves," Chambrun said. He walked around behind his desk, scowling.

"I had no place to go," Constance Cleaves said. "All my things, my family, my life is up there on the fifteenth floor. I thought if I went out there I'd be torn to pieces by questions I can't answer. And if there's any news, it will come here, won't it?"

"Yes, it will come here," Chambrun said. He looked at me. "Care to be a Good Samaritan, Mark?"

I knew what he was asking. The second floor West was occupied by his offices, the business and accounting offices, the hotel telephone switchboard, and at the far end of the hall my office. Also, next to my office, was the two-room apartment in which I live— a sitting room, bedroom, bath, and a tiny kitchenette. Constance Cleaves could be private there and, at the same time, only a few yards from the center of the action, Chambrun's office.

"I'd be pleased to have Mrs. Cleaves hole up in my place," I said.

Chambrun nodded and explained the setup to the woman.

"I can't invade your place, Mr. Haskell," she said.

"Of course you can," I said. "I may have to pop in from time to time for a clean shirt or a change of clothes."

"We can set you up somewhere else, Mark, when there's time for you to move a few things," Chambrun said. "Now, if you'll take Mrs. Cleaves down the hall—" Everything he said made it clear he expected this situation to go on and on. "Mrs. Cleaves will need some personal things—toothbrush, other toilet articles, a change of clothes, night things. You will call the boutique on the main floor, Mrs. Cleaves, and have them send up everything you need, at our expense. It's the least we can do to make up for your discomfort."

"I couldn't think of—"

"See to it, Mark," Chambrun said. "And now I'm afraid I must ask you to leave. We are buried under things to do. Get back as soon as Mrs. Cleaves is settled, Mark."

I took Constance Cleaves down the hall to my apartment. The few people who were still clustered along the way would have stopped her to talk if I had allowed it. I wondered if the floor maid had been to my place or if it would be the usual mess I left it in.

My living room is lined with bookshelves and there are a few nice small paintings I'd acquired from artists who owed me something for services rendered.

"It's so charming," my guest said. "I simply can't allow you to be forced out of here."

"It's really a pleasure to be able to help, Mrs. Cleaves," I said.

She turned to me and there was the hint of tears in her dark blue eyes. "At a time like this one so desperately needs friends," she said, "and this is such a very friendly thing for you to do. I'd like it if you'd call me Connie, Mark. It would help me to feel that I'm not surrounded by strangers and policemen. Oh, God,

Mark, do you think there's any real chance of getting the girls back from these lunatics?''

"Your husband will find the money," I said.

"If that was all! Their other demands—"

"We'll negotiate," I said. "That's the most active verb in the English language today—negotiate."

"No one is going to care about us," she said, her voice breaking. "Their own positions, their own politics, is all that will matter to them. Too bad about two little girls, but they won't turn the world upside-down for them. Doesn't this Coriander creature know that?"

"Money is an important part of his demands," I said. "A hell of a lot of money. That may buy freedom for the girls and Miss Horn. The politics of it are a whole other maneuver." I tried to sound cheerful. "My bed is queen-sized. You and your husband should be able to manage there, and you'll be right next door to any news."

Her lips trembled. "You don't imagine that Terrence will share this place with me—or any place, do you?"

There it was, out in the open.

"Well, I assumed—" I said, or something equally senseless.

"Don't assume anything about Terrence and me, Mark." Suddenly she was hanging onto me, her face buried against my shoulder, her whole body shaken by a struggle against tears. "Can you imagine such a situation—a situation where Liz and Mariella are in the hands of—of a bloody killer—and their parents can't comfort or help each other?"

"Why not?" I asked.

She pulled back from me and lifted her eyes. "Because," she said in a kind of intense whisper, "we loathe each other."

It was not the moment to go into it with her, and she helped make that clear by walking away from me and taking a little tour of the apartment. I showed her where the coffeepot was—and the liquor—and the clean towels.

"I've got to get moving," I said. "If there's anything you need, call my office. It's just next door. And I promise you, if there's any news from upstairs, good or bad, you'll have it the minute after we do."

She was standing beside me near the door, and she reached up and kissed me on the cheek—just a friendly kiss. The subtle scent of her perfume, the closeness of her, tempted me to take my mind off the problems at hand. Some other time, Dad, I told myself. Some other goddamned time.

FOUR

I WENT DOWN the hall to my office, where I found all hell was cooking. There had been a normal schedule of events planned for the day—normal for the Beaumont. There was to have been a luncheon in one of the private dining rooms for a group of United Nations diplomats; a special film showing in our small theater on the second floor North for some big shots in the movie and television world; a lecture in the grand ballroom by Harley Latham, the newest evangelical creep, whose theory was that prayer and positive thinking would not only make you money but supply you with a passport through the heavenly gates; the reading of a new play in one of the private dining rooms by a cast of actors, the playwright, and the director for a group of potential backers or angels; a very private and secret showing of next spring's fashions designed by Audrey Spector, more secret than the plans for the next Middle East war. Someone representing each one of these groups was clamoring for the word from me. Must their meetings be postponed? Would it be safe to go ahead? Everyone wanted to ask the same question at the same time. Just to make things simpler, there were half a dozen people from the press and the media, including the scholarly looking Mr. Colin Andrews, who didn't believe that Terrence Cleaves had three good friends.

I tried to make a general statement that would satisfy everyone. There was no danger on the lower floors of the Beaumont, no reason to postpone.

"What about the pickets outside the hotel?" someone asked.

I didn't know anything about any pickets. Andrews, a faintly bitter smile moving his mouth at the corners, told me what was cooking.

"Release South Vietnam's political victims," he said.

Colonel Coriander was way ahead of us, I thought. There hadn't been time to organize this kind of group in the short time since the news had broken. Coriander had had them ready well in advance. The Army For Justice was for real.

I explained that I had nothing new to tell anyone. Chambrun was satisfied that all the special events could go forward without any danger. People began to drift away. They didn't want to cancel unless it was absolutely necessary. The four girls in my office were all on phones. Hundreds of inquiries were coming through the switchboard and being channeled here.

Colin Andrews of the *London Times* showed no inclination to leave.

"I'd like to talk to you privately," he said.

"There's nothing new," I said.

"Not as a reporter for the *Times*," he said. "It's just possible I might be useful."

Instinct told me he wasn't conning me. I took him into my private office.

"Like two minutes," I told him.

He sat down in the chair beside my desk and lit a cigarette, very carefully, as though it was a scientific experiment.

"Only two minutes to save a human life?" he asked.

"What human life?"

"I should have said 'lives,'" he said. "Katie and the children."

He had a nickname for the sultry Katherine Horn. "So you're another hero," I said.

"Another?" he asked, frowning.

"Douglas Horween," I said. "The spy who came out of the woodwork." I knew I shouldn't have said it the minute it slipped out. If Horween was to try anything, it had to be a secret. And, come to think of it, how did I know that Mr. Colin Andrews wasn't a member of the Army For Justice, working for Coriander on the outside?

"What's his plan?" Andrews asked. His eyes were unblinking behind his wire-rimmed glasses.

"Just big talk—maybe to reassure Mrs. Cleaves," I said.

"Poor Connie," he said.

A friend of the family, I thought. I'd already talked too much, so I glanced at my watch to let him know his two minutes was running out. He didn't seem to notice.

"Do you know what an investigative reporter is?" he asked.

His British accent, rather pleasant, very precise, made him sound patronizing. "I don't have time for word games," I said.

"I want to make the point that I'm not here in the United States on any sort of general assignment," he said. "I'm in the process of preparing some material that will be an exposé of people in very high places in England's politics."

"Don't tell me there's a new call-girl scandal," I said.

"Nothing so amusing," he said. "The story I'm working on is going to blow the lid off in a very big way. I can't talk about it in any detail, but in view of what's happening here I think someone should be made aware of certain facts. It's my feeling that your Mr. Chambrun is the man who would know how to use those facts."

"Your time is about up, Mr. Andrews," I said.

He took a deep drag on his cigarette and let the smoke out in a long sigh. "So I will give you facts," he said. "The Right Honorable Terrence Cleaves is supposed to be a very wealthy man. The fact is that he's on the verge of colossal bankruptcy. It will be one of the great financial scandals of our time. At this moment, for his own purposes, Terrence Cleaves couldn't raise a shilling to make a telephone call."

"That makes it rough for him," I said.

"To hell with him," Andrews said. "The children are the ones who matter. The fact is that Terrence Cleaves needs to raise a huge sum of money to cover his tracks and keep from spending the rest of his life in prison."

"And now he has to raise a second huge sum of money to save his children," I said.

He looked at me, unblinkingly, from behind his faintly tinted glasses. "Think of the possibilities," he said. "He needs to raise millions of pounds to save himself from disgrace and disaster—prison for the rest of his natural life. No one will lend him the money. He has no security left to guarantee a loan of any sort. His property in England is mortgaged to the hilt. Now he has to raise money to ransom his children, and for this, and under the circumstances, he may find people, even governments, willing to help him.''

"But that money, if he can raise it, will go to Coriander and his army," I said.

"Quite so," Andrews said. "You're not as quick on the trigger as I'd hoped you might be, Haskell."

I felt my jaw going slack. "Are you suggesting that Cleaves kidnapped his own children? That he is Coriander?"

"One thing is certain," Andrews said. "Cleaves isn't the one-armed man in the fright wig and mask who told you he was Coriander. Cleaves was at the United Nations while that was going on. I know, because I was covering the meeting of the General Assembly when he got the word from Chambrun. Your Coriander was someone else. But 'Coriander' isn't anyone's real name. Cleaves isn't in this alone, obviously. But fifty million dollars leaves a nice little packet for everyone."

"You're dreaming," I said.

"How were guns and ammunition and explosives smuggled into Cleaves's suite? They couldn't have been brought in overnight by some outside group. They would have been seen by your security people. I suggest they were brought in by Cleaves and his people over a period of time—a box here, a suitcase there. No one would have been suspicious of Cleaves or his people."

"What people?"

"Horween, three male clerks, Katie," Andrews said.

"You're suggesting Miss Horn is in on this?"

"Why not?" Andrews said. His voice was bitter. "He's been screwing her for months."

I leaned back in my chair because I felt weak. "Is that gossip or a fact?"

"Fact," he said. "She was my girl, God help me. She wangled a job taking care of the Cleaves girls so she could get information for me on the inside. Instead of that she wound up in bed with him."

"So you hate him for that," I said.

"I hate him for that," Andrews said, his voice flat and hard. "But I'm out to get him because I think of myself as a decent British subject and this man is planning to sell out his country in order to recoup his private losses."

"So don't hold back your story. Come out in the open with it," I said. "The children aren't in danger if they've been kidnapped by their own father."

"You don't know Terrence Cleaves," Andrews said. He ground out his cigarette in the ash tray beside his chair. "I can't prove my theory—yet—that he is the big man behind all this, the real Coriander. If I hinted at it in public, I don't think he'd stop at anything to get the money and escape to some sanctuary. He doesn't give a damn for the children, or for Connie. If I blast him publicly, I'd have to live the rest of my bloody life with whatever he does to the girls or his wife or to Katie on my conscience."

"And what do you expect Chambrun to do?"

"Check out on the sketch I've drawn for you," Andrews said. "He has top-level contacts all over the world. He'll come across other people who have doubts and suspicions about Terrence Cleaves."

"Suppose he does. What can he do about it? He can't risk the lives of those children and Miss Horn, or the guests in his hotel, or the hotel itself. He's handcuffed. Everybody is handcuffed. So we all sit around and chew on your little bit of gossip and wait for the negotiations with Coriander to begin. We can't act on anything, even if you're right about Cleaves. Tell me something, will you?"

"If I can."

"Is it Cleaves's affair with your Miss Horn that has wrecked his marriage to Connie?"

"His affair with Katie and God knows how many others," Andrews said.

"Why does she stay with him?" I asked. "The children?"

"I doubt that," he said, as though it was something he'd thought about before. "If she walked out on him, the courts would surely give her custody of the children. Cleaves's woman chasing is one thing that's public knowledge. I think he's got some other kind of hold on her. I've tried to dig out what it might be, but I've had no luck."

I stood up. "I'll pass along your story to Chambrun," I said.

He didn't move. It was as if the telling of the story had exhausted him. "You saw Katie when you had your session with Coriander?" he asked.

"I saw her. She seemed quite cool."

He brought his hand down hard on the arm of his chair. "Why not?" he said, his voice harsh. "She knows she's in no danger!"

MR. JAMES PRIEST from the State Department was in Chambrun's office when I got back there. I knew him, slightly, as a frequent guest at the Beaumont. He always stayed with us when he came to New York, quite often on United Nations business. He was a big, easy-going man, who made you feel comfortable with a quick humor and a sense of relaxed control of himself and complete self-confidence in his ability to handle his specialty, diplomatic maneuvering. You had the feeling he was thoroughly familiar with every highway and byway and side street and cul-de-sac in his business.

He was relaxed in one of Chambrun's big green leather armchairs, a pipe held between his strong white teeth, the light from the north windows shining on his sun-tanned bald head. He gave me a little wave of a hand as I came in.

"It looks as though this Coriander fellow has taken over your job, Mark," he said. "He seems to be keeping the press informed. I just walked through the picket lines and the crowds out on the street."

"He's certainly well organized," I said. I glanced at Chambrun, who was sipping his inevitable Turkish coffee. "Things are pretty well under control," I told him. "We haven't had a single cancellation of any special events."

"Jim would like to hear a detailed account of your visit with Coriander," Chambrun said. "It seems there are no records in any official departments—the FBI, the CIA, anywhere else—of an Army For Justice. It could almost have been invented for this purpose."

"Those pickets outside the hotel didn't just grow like Topsy," I said. "They were ready the minute Coriander let the news out."

Priest nodded, puffing gently on his pipe. "This Army can have been in existence for some time," he said. "The reason there are no reports or records on them is that this is the first time they've made any sort of public display. They've undoubtedly been preparing for the big one and keeping under cover so that there was no chance we could anticipate them. Tell me about Coriander, Mark."

"Before I do that I'd like to pass on a theory that's just been given to me," I said. "Do you know of an English newspaperman named Colin Andrews, Mr. Priest?"

"Oh, yes," Priest said. "One of the top political reporters in his country."

"He's for real?"

"Very much for real," Priest said. "British politicos keep their fingers well out of the cookie jar when Andrews is on the horizon. He has a very keen nose for secret shenanigans."

"You remember him?" I said to Chambrun. "He's the one who suggested Cleaves didn't have three friends. Well, he's got another theory about Cleaves."

I gave it to them from top to bottom. Neither one of them spoke till I had finished. They were a couple of dead-pan artists, those two.

Chambrun looked at Priest, an eyebrow raised, when I'd finished. That look was a question.

Priest's pipe had gone out and he lit it with a jet-flame lighter. "It's a pretty bizarre notion," he said. "But there is a little smoke to justify the suggestion of a hidden fire. I don't think it's any great secret that Cleaves has had some financial problems. I imagine that you both know he was—is—something of a sports hero in Britain: cricketer, international polo player, crack amateur golfer. He was also a fighter pilot, a top ace, in the R.A.F. in World War Two. A hero figure in both areas. His name would sell almost any product he chose to lend it to. A few years ago he went into the manufacture of high-priced sports cars. I believe he actually drove one of the prototypes at Le Mans. It was called the T.C. 4, his initials. Most, if not all, of the seed money came from him. The T.C. 4 came on the market at just the wrong time—inflation, fuel shortages, tight money. It was a complete bust. It was no secret that Terry Cleaves lost several million pounds—a hell of a lot of money. But that kind of loss is relative in a very rich man. If I lost ten million dollars, assuming I'd ever had any such amount, I'd be dead broke. In Cleaves's case he was said to have lost about that much and found himself left with only five million! Not exactly broke, if you see what I mean. Everybody bought him drinks and said 'Bad luck, old chap,' but, secretly, nobody felt too sorry for him. He was still stinking rich."

"The losses could have been greater than anybody knew," Chambrun said.

"Possibly," Priest said. "I said there was a little smoke." His pipe had gone out again and he relit it. "The other smoky area is a little odd in view of what Andrews told you, Mark. I've never heard a whisper about Cleaves's sex life. Would I if he was screwing around? I think I would, under the circumstances. When the British Government wanted to send him to the United Nations as their ambassador, they discussed it with us. That wasn't an unusual procedure. We work very closely with the British at the U.N. There was one reason to make us hesitate. It was rumored that Constance Cleaves, the proposed ambassador's wife, was scandalously indiscreet in her sex habits. Not Cleaves, you understand, but the lady."

I was astonished to discover that I wanted to do battle for the lady with the copper-colored hair, but I kept my mouth shut.

"Constance Cleaves comes from a pretty colorful background herself," Priest said. "She's American, the daughter of Walter Ames. Buck Ames, they call him, and the Buck is a contraction of Buccaneer. Pirate."

"He's some sort of lobbyist, isn't he?" Chambrun asked.

"Duly registered, perfectly legitimate lobbyist for ITC, the International Trade Corporation," Priest said. "He's a big, jovial, delightful, outrageous wheeler and dealer. He's welcomed in the best homes in the capital cities all over the world. When Buck Ames is at a party, it *is* a party. His wife died giving birth to Constance, and Constance is the apple of his eye, to coin a cliché. As a young girl she was just as wildly outrageous as her father. She chased all over the map of the globe, involved as a teenager with all the young and middle-aged eligible bachelors on the scene. She was said to have been in the hay with most of them. Cleaves, the national hero of Great Britain, was her climax, and one worthy of her. She married him and settled down to bear him two children. Her life style changed but the gossip lingered on."

"Buck Ames has money, no?" Chambrun asked.

"And spends it like water," Priest said. "But I should have thought he would have been the first person Cleaves would go to for help. Buck's contacts are the best in the world."

I could hear Connie's husky voice saying, "We loathe each other." If she hated her husband, that probably meant her adoring father hated him, too. But Elizabeth and Mariella were his grandchildren. Surely the buccaneer would come to bat for them.

"You wanted to make a guess on Andrews' theory, Jim?" Chambrun asked.

Priest knocked his pipe out in the ash tray beside his chair. "It's an ingenious one," he said. "It's the kind of theory I'd expect to come out of the kind of mind Colin Andrews has. Complex, devious. He could be working out a grudge if Cleaves stole his girl from him. He would like it to be Cleaves."

"He could be working for Coriander on the outside, throwing dust in our faces," I said.

"I'd have vouched for Andrews' honesty," Priest said.

"Fifty million bucks can buy a hell of a lot of honesty," I said. "I can't buy the idea that Cleaves, no matter how cold his guts are, would consider mutilating his own children."

"Nobody has mutilated them yet," Chambrun said. "So far it's only a threat." He pushed away his coffee cup with a kind of decisive gesture. "It's rather fun to sit here playing guessing games, but let's get down to the hard core of the problem. Coriander, whoever he is, has made demands. He knows it will take a little while for any sort of answers to come his way. The money has to be raised, and that, despite the amount, is the easiest part of it. Cleaves can raise it or he can't. He'll get offers of help whether he has friends or not. If he can't raise it all, he makes a counterproposal. But unless Coriander is playing games with us, the far more important answer for him is whether the political prisoners in Vietnam can be released."

Priest laughed, a mirthless sound. "Do I have to tell you the answer to that, Pierre?"

"Horween was right," Chambrun said. "We'd have to send the United States Army back there to make that happen."

"If you have lived in the world of bargaining, as I have most of my life," Priest said, "you know that the most elementary technique is to ask for more than you expect to get. Coriander has to know that there is no way we can free thousands of prisoners. But in the end it might be possible to get certain key people freed. Those key people may be what he's interested in. As for trying higher-ups for war crimes—" Priest shrugged. "It would take months and months for any such trials to take place, and Coriander isn't going to sit up there on the fifteenth floor waiting for that to happen. No, my guess is he has some special friends in those tiger cages in Vietnam—politicians, newspaper editors, genuine revolutionaries—who will satisfy him. The money will help to finance his total cause. Those two things are what it's all about."

"You don't buy the idea that the whole thing is a hoax and that it's all a scheme of Terrence Cleaves's to refinance himself?" I asked.

Priest gave me a benign, paternal smile. "I don't really buy it, Mark," he said, "but I don't intend to ignore it as a possibility. Ask your friend Andrews if he'd care to talk to me—in confidence. We'll do some checking out with our connections in Britain."

"We can't touch him in the process," Chambrun said. "He isn't the one-armed man you saw upstairs, Mark. We know where he was when you were talking to Coriander. We can't play a ponderous chess game with this situation. We're sitting, quite literally, on a time bomb. That bastard upstairs may choose at any minute to lop off a little girl's ear just to show us he means business. What we need, Jim, is a big statement from the government that they're trying to work out something on his demands. We need a public statement from Cleaves that he's working to raise the money. Meanwhile, God help us, we've got to decide what we're going to do if none of the demands can be met. We've got to plan some kind of a one-shot strike that has a possibility of getting those children out of there in one piece. It has to work, because we'll never get a second chance.''

At that moment the office door opened and Ruysdale came in. She had a kind of odd, strained look on her face.

''I'm sorry to interrupt,'' she said, ''but there's a man named Fritz Schindler outside who's a waiter on the room service. He says it's urgent that he talk to you, Mr. Chambrun.''

Chambrun sat up very straight in his chair. ''Have the room service people served the lunch order on the fifteenth floor?'' he asked.

''About twenty minutes ago,'' Ruysdale said. ''I think this man may have seen something, or has a message for you from Coriander.''

''Bring him in,'' Chambrun said.

Chambrun knows every member of our huge staff by sight, by name, by his or her history in our employment records. I recognized Fritz Schindler when he came in—a tall, stooped old man with snow-white hair, a big beak of a nose, and pale eyes that watered behind rimless spectacles. He was wearing black trousers, a white shirt with black tie, and a scarlet waiter's jacket. He was often part of the crew that served at special banquets or luncheons in the private dining rooms. He spoke in a rather husky voice with a thick German accent.

"Forgive me for intruding, Mr. Chambrun," he said.

"It's quite all right, Fritz," Chambrun said. "You have just served a food order on the fifteenth floor?"

"Ja," Fritz said. "Thirty servings."

"You have a message for me, or you saw something that would interest me?"

"Not that, Mr. Chambrun. I am disturbed about something else."

"Let's have it, Fritz."

"Late this morning Miss Ruysdale brought a man down to the kitchens while we were preparing the food for Fifteen A. His name is Horween, and he is registered in 1507. I have served him there."

"Go on."

"He seemed to take a special interest in me. He had a little camera and he took—what do you call them?—candid shots of me. He explained that someone might try to take my place the next time there was an order. Someone made up to look like me. That is what bothers me, Mr. Chambrun."

"Such a plan has been discussed, Fritz," Chambrun said.

"Before I would back away and let someone take my place, I have to have the order direct from you, Mr. Chambrun. I would not take such an order from anyone else. I would be betraying the trust you place in me."

Chambrun leaned back in his chair and a slow smile lighted his face. "That's really very good, Mr. Horween," he said. "Really terribly good."

The old waiter straightened up. "Damn! I'd have sworn you couldn't tell," he said, the German accent gone.

My eyes were popping out of my head. It was Horween, and I'd have sworn it was Fritz Schindler. The man was a genius at disguise, which is exactly what he'd told us.

"Don't be downhearted," Chambrun said, still smiling. "I probably would have fallen for it if it hadn't been for Ruysdale. She can never hide a deception from me, perhaps because she's had so little practice."

Horween took off the rimless glasses and wiped his eyes with a tissue. "Glycerine," he said, in his clipped British voice, "designed to give me that rheumy look."

"I'm satisfied you might get away with it," Chambrun said. The smile disappeared. "But I want to make it quite clear to you, Horween, that you're not to try anything on your own without permission from me. It could interfere with some plan of our own, and to drop the ball, just once, could produce a tragedy."

"What plan?" Horween asked.

"If it's to include you, you will be told," Chambrun said. "I'll have your hide, Horween, if you try anything on your own."

I REMEMBER THINKING, as I left Chambrun's office, that maybe warnings weren't enough for Horween. I had the feeling he was the kind of character who would make his own decisions, and to hell with what anyone told him to do or not to do. But I had other things on my mind and so I forgot about him at that time. Chambrun's judgments were usually sound. Invariably sound, I would have said if I'd been asked.

What was on my mind was the gal with the copper-colored hair who was down the hall in my apartment. Jim Priest wasn't a backstairs gossip. He wouldn't have said that Connie Cleaves had been scandalously indiscreet about her sex habits unless there was some substance to the rumor. Chambrun would have kicked my ass all the way down Fifth Avenue if he'd guessed at the idea that was starting to percolate in the back of my head. She was such a very damned attractive doll.

Good old loyal Mark Haskell decided he'd better stop by the apartment and see if the lady had everything she needed. I knocked on the door, first gently, and then hard. There wasn't any answer, so I used my key. Just inside the door I called out, with a kind of false cheerfulness, "It's me. Mark."

It took only a few seconds for me to discover that Connie Cleaves wasn't in the apartment. There were some packages on the couch that had come from the boutique in the lobby. She'd ordered things, as Chambrun had suggested, but she hadn't bothered to open the packages.

I was disappointed but not terribly concerned. She wasn't a prisoner. She had a right to go and come as she pleased. She was the one who had wanted protection from the press and other curious people. If she chose to face them, it was her business. Still—

I picked up the phone and got Mrs. Veach, the chief operator on the hotel switchboard. I asked her if there had been any incoming or outgoing calls on my phone in the last hour.

There was no record of anything. They don't keep records of calls made from one room to another in the hotel. An out-call would be recorded because the room would be charged for it. There is no record of in-calls, unless there is a message left or an inquiry made.

"You're monitoring calls to and from Fifteen A?" I asked Mrs. Veach.

"Everything, in and out," Mrs. Veach said.

"And there was nothing from Fifteen to my room, or the other way around?"

"We'd have that if there had been," the good lady told me.

It had occurred to me that Connie might have called Coriander to plead for a chance to speak to her children, or that he might have called her to impress on her that he wasn't kidding. How would he know that she was in my apartment? I had the uncomfortable feeling he knew everything that was going on in the hotel.

Well, she would be back, I told myself. But, as I headed about my routine business—because Chambrun insisted that things must be running smoothly— I made a few casual checks. Johnny Thacker, the day bell captain, hadn't seen her in the lobby. She wasn't in the Trapeze Bar or the main dining room or the Grill. She had taken a walk, and when she was ready she would walk back—I told myself.

It wasn't an afternoon I am likely to forget. In addition to the routines of checking on the special events, making certain that everything was running smoothly, I was hounded by everybody who laid eyes on me for the latest on the big story. There wasn't anything new to tell, so far as I knew. I was aware of comings and goings. I saw Gus Brand, the FBI man, headed for Chambrun's office in midafternoon and I managed to flag him down. Had he found out anything about the Army For Justice and Coriander?

"The Army seems to be new as far as our records are concerned," he told me. "The CIA draws a blank on it, too. Our best unofficial contacts also draw a blank."

"Yet there are a couple of hundred of them milling up and down out on the sidewalk," I said.

"There always has to be a first exposure," Brand said.

"Coriander?" I asked him.

His face hardened. "The number of amputees out of Vietnam would make you sick at your stomach," he said. "It's going to take a long time to check out on how many lost an arm, and specifically a left arm. By the time we come up with an answer, the ball game may be over."

Later on while I was passing through the lobby, I saw Johnny Thacker guiding a three-star general toward Chambrun's office. The Pentagon was obviously responding to the outrageous notion that they should be held responsible for civilian massacres in Indochina carried out by some young punk lieutenants.

Valentine, the big, gray bomb squad man, was very much in evidence, and the hotel was generally swarming with men who couldn't be anything else but cops. Late in the afternoon I called Ruysdale to ask her if Cleaves had reported back with a hatful of money.

"He's called in," Ruysdale told me. "He's working on it. He made it sound as though the going was tough."

"Anything from Mrs. Cleaves?"

"She's in your apartment, isn't she?"

"She's gone somewhere," I said.

I have to admit I'd called my rooms on the house phones a few times. No answer.

Just before six o'clock we had a small riot in the lobby. A couple of dozen of the pickets, all young males and females, long-haired, bearded, navels bared, barged in carrying their signs. FREE THE VIETNAM POLITICAL PRISONERS. JUSTICE IN THE PENTAGON. THE SINS OF THE FATHER SHOULD NOT BE PAID FOR BY HIS CHILDREN. PEACE WITH HONOR FOR REAL. LET THE RIGHT PEOPLE LIVE AND THE WRONG PEOPLE DIE.

These young people, screaming and yelling, gave us a picture of how tight the security was. They'd hardly got through the door from the street when they were surrounded by an army of cops, some uniformed, some in plain clothes, and a dozen of Jerry Dodd's hotel security people. They were swept back out onto the street so fast they must have thought they'd been hit by a cyclone. The hotel guests must have wondered if they'd really seen what they'd seen.

About six-thirty I went back up to my apartment and tried knocking. There was no answer, so I let myself in with my key again. The place was just as I'd left it a few hours back: the unopened packages from the boutique on the couch, and no Connie. I was beginning to be genuinely anxious about her, and not on account of my possible love life. I decided I'd go down the hall and report this matter to Chambrun, but just as I reached the door, my phone rang.

It was Chambrun. "You're wanted," he said.

"On my way," I said.

"Not here," he said in a flat voice that I knew spelled trouble. "Fifteen A. Coriander wants you on the double. There's something wrong, Mark."

"What?"

"No idea. He won't talk to anyone but you in person."

"Have we got anything for him?" I asked. "Money? Concessions?"

"Nothing yet."

"I was just coming to tell you that Constance Cleaves has taken a powder on me. She's been missing for about four hours. She ordered stuff from the boutique but she didn't stop to open the packages."

"You come on too strong?" he asked.

"What are you talking about?"

"I know you, Mark. I know you. Jim Priest's remarks about the lady opened new vistas for you."

"She'd gone before I could make an ass of myself," I said.

"Get upstairs as quickly as you can," Chambrun said. "Coriander could explode if you keep him waiting."

And so, with my heart beating rather unpleasantly against my ribs, I headed upstairs. I took the elevator to 16 and walked down. One of Jerry Dodd's men checked on my right to be on the fire stairs.

The fifteenth floor was deserted, just as it had been on my first visit. I walked to the door of 15 A and knocked. The door was opened promptly, not by Coriander, but by one of the men wearing a stocking mask. He waved me in without speaking.

A second man wearing a stocking mask was sitting, very relaxed, on a straight chair tilted back against the wall. He had a machine pistol resting on his lap, one hand caressing it as though it was a live pet. Coriander, in his Halloween mask and his fright wig, was standing behind a stretcher table in the center of the room, the left sleeve of his red dressing gown hanging limply at his side. In front of him on the table was a bulky package wrapped in newspapers.

"I warned you, Haskell," he said. "No tricks." His voice was shaken by a fierce anger I hadn't heard there before.

"What tricks?" I asked him. "I don't know about any tricks."

"It surprises me that Chambrun would try anything so amateurish," he said. He gestured with his good arm at the package on the table. "Open it."

I stepped forward and pulled the newspapers away from what they covered. I felt a trickle of sweat running down my back. What I saw was a pile of clothes: underwear, a white shirt, a black tie, black shoes, black trousers, and a bright scarlet waiter's jacket. The shirt and the undershirt were stained with what looked like blood. Then I saw something else, buried under the garments. It was a white wig. There was also a pair of rimless spectacles and a wallet.

"Did your master-minding boss imagine I couldn't detect an obvious disguise?" Coriander asked.

Horween, I thought. He had made his move in spite of all orders.

"The stupid son of a bitch even carried his own wallet," Coriander said. "Douglas Horween, the alleged master spy in the employ of Cleaves. Did any of you really imagine he could pull off some kind of stunt, or report back to you on our defenses?"

"Where is he?" I asked, my voice sounding weak and reedy.

"He is dead!" Coriander almost shouted. "He has, you might say, gone down the drain. I want you to take that bundle of clothes back to Chambrun and tell him the man's blood, which you can see on his shirt, is on his head. And tell him that one more miserable trick of this sort and the blood of one of the little girls will also be on his head. One more stroke of genius like this and we'll really go into action. Now, pick up that package and go!"

I fumbled with the papers, my fingers stiff and clumsy. Any uncertainty about Coriander's capacity for violence was dissolved. Now we had a murder on our hands.

"Horween acted on his own," I managed to say, "against strict orders from Mr. Chambrun."

"I almost believe you," Coriander said, "because this was far too stupid for Chambrun to have approved. But tell him I hold him responsible for any fun and games anyone tries up here."

Somehow I managed to gather up the package and got the hell out of there.

PART TWO

PART TWO

ONE

LIEUTENANT HARDY of Manhattan's Homicide Squad was an old friend of ours. The Beaumont had had its murders over the years and Hardy had handled several of them, had come to respect Chambrun and Jerry Dodd, and the feeling was reciprocated.

Hardy looks more like a big, good-natured, slightly puzzled all-pro fullback than a highly efficient expert in the field of homicide. He moves slowly, but with a kind of dogged stubbornness. No flash of genius carries him past any given fact until he has worked it over, shaken it out, dissected it. There are never any loose ends on Hardy's back-trail.

There is a brief, nightmare period in my memory. I don't recall who I saw or may have spoken to on my way down from 15 A to Chambrun's office, carrying that ghastly bundle wrapped in newspaper. I remember thinking I could feel the wetness of blood seeping through onto my hands, but of course I couldn't and didn't. I remember lunging past Ruysdale in her outer office and arriving at Chambrun's desk where I, dramatically, threw the package down in front of him. He looked at me, startled. I guess I must have been the color of a pale pea soup.

"What the hell is this?" he said.

"Horween," I said, and sat down in the leather chair facing him because my knees were buckling under me.

Chambrun stared at me as if I'd gone out of my mind, and then, gingerly, he unwrapped the package. One by one he examined the articles he found: the shirt, the underthings, the pants, the jacket, the shoes, the tie, the white wig, the rimless glasses, the wallet. No need to explain to him what the scarlet stains on the shirt and undershirt were. Through a kind of fog I saw him pick up the wallet and thumb through it. Then he was reaching for the phone and I heard him telling Ruysdale to try to get Lieutenant Hardy at Homicide.

Then he did something I can never remember his doing before or since. He walked over to the sideboard, poured a very stiff slug of Jack Daniel's, neat, and brought it over to me. People always waited on him; reversing the role was an historic moment which I wasn't really able to enjoy.

"Drink this and get pulled together," he said. He stood in front of me while I downed the whiskey and then took the glass away from me. "You saw the body?"

I shook my head.

"Then you don't know for certain—?"

"He told me," I said. "Down the drain."

"Down the drain?"

"That's what he told me."

Chambrun had moved to his desk. I heard him ask that Fritz Schindler and whoever had served anything to 15 A since lunch should report at once. At that point Jerry Dodd came into the office. I guess he looked at me, I'm not sure. The whiskey felt hot in my gut, but things were still a little foggy.

Jerry was going through the things in the package. I saw him take something out of the wallet.

"He carried a blood-type card," Jerry said. "AB negative. Not too usual. If the bloodstains on the shirt match—" He shrugged. I saw that, so evidently I was coming around.

"We need it from the top, Mark," Chambrun said.

I told them exactly what had happened; the armed men in stocking masks, Coriander's anger, his threats, his warnings.

"What did you think he meant by 'down the drain'?"

"Hack it to pieces, a little acid, and gurgle, gurgle," Jerry Dodd said. "We better get Fritz Schindler and whoever else served drinks or supper to Fifteen A. In spite of what you told him, Horween obviously took Schindler's place."

Chambrun didn't act, but I realized the intercom was on and that Betsy Ruysdale was already doing what he wanted done. Her voice came through to us after a moment.

"There were drinks ordered about five-thirty," she told us. "According to Room Service, Schindler and a waiter named Edward Sprague delivered the order. They're both still on duty and are on their way up. And Lieutenant Hardy should be here in a few minutes."

"Thanks, Ruysdale," Chambrun said.

"You notified the police?" Jerry asked the boss.

Chambrun nodded.

"You don't know yet if you've got a homicide," Jerry said. "Just some clothes, a bloodstained shirt, and some articles of disguise. You got to have a body they always say."

"Horween was wearing all those articles of clothing and disguise not too long ago," Chambrun said.

"And we have his wallet. If we don't have a homicide, we'll buy Hardy a drink and send him home."

The real Fritz Schindler jolted me when he came into the office along with Edward Sprague, who looked a little like an ex-prize fighter. The white-haired Schindler, rheumy eyes behind his rimless spectacles, was an exact replica of the phony Schindler that Horween had tried to pass off on us. When he spoke in his slow German accent, the total sameness was astonishing. Horween had been some kind of genius.

"I hope there is nothing wrong, Mr. Chambrun," Schindler said.

"What could be wrong, Fritz?" Chambrun asked.

"My letting Mr. Horween take my place," he said. "I mean—" And then he saw the stuff lying on Chambrun's desk and his mouth dropped open.

"Something may have happened to Mr. Horween," Chambrun said.

Schindler muttered something under his breath in German. Then: "I was sure it was in accordance with your wishes, Mr. Chambrun. Miss Ruysdale brought him down late this morning. She said I was to cooperate in every way with Mr. Horween."

"How did you cooperate, Fritz?"

"He took some candid snapshots of me. Mostly he talked to me, and after a while he was talking back to me. It was amazing. He sounded just like me. Then he borrowed my extra set of clothes, my extra uniform, and he went away. A little before six he came back to Room Service and I swear I thought I was looking in a mirror."

"I would never of known if I hadn't seen them standing together," Sprague said.

"You saw them together, Ed?" Chambrun asked. "Who else saw them?"

"I dunno. Two or three others. I was in our locker room."

"So Coriander could have known before Horween ever started up there," Jerry Dodd said. "Can you remember who those two or three others were, Sprague?"

"I'm not sure," Sprague said. "One of 'em was Georges Makroupolis, the Greek. I—I was so stunned by the lookalikes I didn't notice who else. I remember I said, 'Will the real Fritz Schindler step forward.' You know, like the TV show? And, God, they both stepped forward."

"And somebody warned Coriander," Jerry said. "I better get on that, Mr. Chambrun. Find out if Makroupolis remembers who else was there."

Chambrun nodded and Jerry left us.

"Now, Fritz and Ed, I want to know exactly what happened. I want to know what the order was that went upstairs and what happened when you got up there," Chambrun said.

Fritz Schindler shook his head. "I can't tell you anything, Mr. Chambrun, because, you see, I didn't go. While we were marveling at Mr. Horween's disguise, the order came over the loud-speaker in the locker room for me and Sprague to prepare an order for Fifteen A. Drinks, the room service captain said. Mr. Horween said that was his moment and he and Edward left me in the locker room."

"The order was all drinks," Sprague said. "Two dozen glasses, ice, four six-packs of imported beer, two bottles of Scotch, two gins, tonic water. It took two service wagons to carry it up."

"The captain didn't notice anything wrong about the man he thought was Schindler?"

Sprague laughed. "This Horween didn't know where anything was, of course. I had to find everything for him. The captain asked him what's the matter with you, he asked him. And Mr. Horween, sounding exactly like Schindler, said he was scared shitless to go up to Fifteen A. That seemed to satisfy the captain. So finally we wheeled the two wagons onto the service elevator and went up to Fifteen."

"Nobody stopped you or checked on you?" Chambrun asked.

"Oh, one of the hotel security people was running the elevator. We usually run the elevator for ourselves, but since the scare on Fifteen this morning, there's been a security man."

"So you went up to Fifteen."

"Yes, sir. And we wheeled the wagons to the door of Fifteen A and knocked. This fellow wearing a mask opened the door."

"A Halloween mask and a fright wig?"

Sprague frowned. "I didn't see anyone like that, Mr. Chambrun."

"A man with an arm missing?"

"I didn't see anyone like that, sir. This man was wearing like a stocking mask. I've seen crooks wear them on television. He was carrying some kind of automatic gun. He told us to bring the wagons in."

"Who else was there?"

"No one," Sprague said. "I forgot to mention there was two bottles of Coca-Cola in the order. He told Mr. Horween—though he called him Schindler—to mix a gin and tonic and two Cokes in glasses with ice and take them into the back room to the ladies."

"He called him Schindler?"

"Sure. They knew our names the first time we went up there with the lunch order, Schindler and me. This guy says, 'Schindler, you mix a gin and tonic and two Cokes in glasses with ice and take them to the ladies in the rear right bedroom. And you, Sprague, unload the wagons and put the stuff on that center table!'"

"So Horween made the gin and tonic and the two glasses of Coke?"

"Yeah. I guess he didn't have to be a real waiter to know how to do that. He made the drinks while I was unloading the wagons and took them down the corridor to the bedroom. The guy in the mask closed the door behind him. When I'd finished unloading, he told me to take both wagons and beat it. I told him it would be awkward for me to handle both wagons. He told me to take 'em out into the hall and he didn't give a damn what happened to them after that.

"'Let Schindler bring one of 'em,' I said. I was worried about Mr. Horween."

"'Schindler is going to stay here and make drinks for us,' he said. 'You beat it.' And so I had no choice but to leave him there while I took the two wagons out to the service elevator and came back downstairs. Mr. Horween never did come back to Room Service."

"Because they spotted him for a fake and may have killed him," Chambrun said.

"God!"

The office door opened and Betsy Ruysdale ushered in Lieutenant Hardy.

HARDY HAD, of course, heard the news on the radio or TV about the kidnapping and the bomb threat.

"I figured I might be seeing you sooner or later," he said.

He listened to a composite of all our stories, looking over the garments and the disguise things on Chambrun's desk as we talked.

"According to this card in his wallet his blood type is AB negative," Chambrun said. "That's fairly rare, isn't it?"

"About three percent of the population," Hardy said. "If these bloodstains turn out to be AB negative, we have a presumption." He held up the bloody shirt. "You have to look twice to see what may have made the wound. A tiny hole in the shirt and in the undershirt. Something like an ice pick or an awl. Something that could have penetrated deep enough to go straight into the heart."

The two waiters had gone and Chambrun, Hardy and I were alone.

"The trouble is, my friend," Hardy said in his quiet way, "there isn't much I can do about it under the circumstances. The laboratory can go over these things. Not much chance for fingerprints except on the shoes, possibly the glasses, possibly the sweat band inside the wig. They'll probably turn out to be Horween's if there are any. Of course there's a chance we might find others. Every piece of silverware, every glass, every plate that comes out of the fifteenth floor should be checked. If this Army For Justice is made up of ex-service men, there are records we can use for crosschecking purposes. But we don't have proof of a homicide—not yet."

"If the blood type matches?" Chambrun said.

"Presumption. We can presume that Douglas Horween bled. That doesn't prove he is dead. It would be enough—all of it would be enough—to justify an investigation under normal circumstances. But tell me how I investigate? I can't go up to Fifteen without risking harm to the girls and Miss Horn; or risk your hotel being blown up over your head. Right now, we don't have a body, we don't have access. Horween may be alive, but another hostage, to be used later. He may have been wounded trying to fight off Coriander and his people, which would account for the blood, the probable wound. But we don't have any proof of death, and even if we did—'' He shrugged.

The phone on Chambrun's desk blinked its red eye. He picked up the receiver and said, ''Yes?''

It turned out to be Cleaves, waiting in the outer office. Chambrun had him come in. The Englishman looked gray with fatigue. He acknowledged the introduction to Hardy with a vague nod of his head.

''Any news?'' he asked.

Chambrun gestured toward the bloody clothes. ''Horween,'' he said. ''He disobeyed orders and substituted for one of our waiters. Coriander says he is dead, and sent us these things to prove it.''

''Oh, my God,'' Cleaves said. He sank down into one of the leather armchairs. ''He was such a crazy, brave idiot!''

''Do you have any news?'' Chambrun asked.

''Nothing positive. Friends are trying to work out ways and means.''

''Do you know where your wife is?'' Chambrun asked. He hadn't forgotten about Connie.

Cleaves shook his head as though it was a matter of no concern. ''I haven't the foggiest,'' he said.

''Mark put her up in his apartment down the hall,'' Chambrun said. ''She walked out some hours ago and she hasn't reappeared. I wondered if you might know where she could have gone?''

"No, and what does it matter?" Cleaves said.

"It occurred to me that she might have tried to join the children," Chambrun said, "and that she may have become another hostage."

"That doesn't alter my problem, which is raising the money," Cleaves said.

"Another thought I had was that she might have gone to her father for help."

That seemed to wake Cleaves up a little. "Buck Ames? He wouldn't help me to buy a fish-and-chips if I was starving."

"They are his grandchildren!" Chambrun said, suddenly angry. "Look here, Cleaves, I don't know what's wrong between you and your wife, but I think it may be important for us to know."

"It's none of your bloody business," Cleaves said.

"But you concede it's possible your wife may have gone to her father for help?"

"Anything is possible where Constance and Buck Ames are concerned."

"What do you mean by that?"

"I mean they are pea-pod close. I mean they would both enjoy seeing me hang from the highest tree. I mean they would spring the trap under my feet if they could. Fortunately, they can't."

"Where can we find Ames?"

"How the bloody hell should I know?"

"If your wife went to find him, it suggests he might be somewhere here in the city. I find it difficult to believe she'd go too far away from the hotel and her children."

"If there is a young and eager stud around some-where, that's probably where you'll find her," Cleaves said. And he looked at me. "She's staying in your apartment, Haskell?" He gave me a very white, very mirthless smile. I would have enjoyed wiping it off his face, but I had the unhappy feeling he could beat the bewadding out of me.

"Does Ames have an apartment or an office here in New York?" Chambrun persisted, ignoring the cracks about Connie.

Cleaves seemed to sink back into his private con-cerns. "I believe there is a secretary somewhere, in someone's office, who takes messages for him."

"International Trade Corporation?"

"A private phone, I think."

"What office, what secretary?"

"I believe the phone for Ames is listed under the single name Buccaneer."

Chambrun nodded to me and I began thumbing through the phone book. There it was—Buccaneer. I wrote down the number and handed it to Chambrun.

"Try it," he said to me.

"Offices will be closed," I said. "It's going on seven o'clock."

"Try it."

I dialed the number and it resulted in an almost im-mediate answer from a pleasant female voice that said, "Buccaneer."

I handed the phone to Chambrun and he switched on the squawk box so we could all hear. "This is Pi-erre Chambrun, manager of the Hotel Beaumont," he said. "I'm trying to reach Walter Ames."

"I'm sorry, Mr. Chambrun, but I'm not allowed to give out any information about Mr. Ames."

"If you've been listening to the news at any time today, you know that his grandchildren are in big trouble."

"I know. Is there any fresh news?"

"I'm not allowed to give out any information about the case," Chambrun said.

The girl on the other end laughed. "I'm sorry; I wish I could help."

"Has Mrs. Cleaves been in touch with you in the last few hours?" Chambrun asked.

The girl hesitated. "I think I have to say 'no' to that," she said, which was a rather neat way of saying "yes."

"Do you have any way of guessing where she might be?"

Again the hesitation. "She may have gone to Athens to see her father."

"Athens!"

"I'm afraid that's the only suggestion I can make, Mr. Chambrun. And now if you'll excuse me—" The phone clicked off.

"That's crazy!" I said. "She wouldn't go to Athens, with her kids locked up by a madman on the fifteenth floor."

"The world has shrunk," Chambrun said. "She could go to Athens and back in a day if she felt her father's help was critical."

Cleaves leaned back in his chair and laughed—a strange hollow sound. "On the west shore of the Hudson River, a hundred or more miles from New York, is a town called Athens. Buck Ames was born there. His father ran a whorehouse in an old railroad hotel there back in the twenties. Constance's grandmother was a very glamorous madam. Connie inherited her taste for promiscuity. I believe Buck Ames has a cottage in Athens, New York, that he visits out of nostalgia for the good old days." He stood up. "I don't have time to worry about Buck or Connie. I've got to find money. You suggested I talk to the State Department man who was coming."

"James Priest. He's registered here in the hotel."

"Would your secretary find out if he could see me?"

Chambrun picked up his phone and asked Ruysdale to locate Jim Priest. He was in his room and quite willing to talk to Cleaves. When we were alone, Hardy spoke for the first time.

"What's all that got to do with the price of eggs?" he asked.

"I think perhaps we'd better find out," Chambrun said.

"What gives with this man and his wife?" Hardy asked.

"We have two stories," Chambrun said. He gave Hardy the Andrews theory and the gossip passed on by Jim Priest. "One way or another, the marriage is evidently held together by hate."

"A strange kind of glue," Hardy said.

"Whatever else, Constance Cleaves's concern for her two young daughters seemed very real to me," Chambrun said. "I'm concerned that she's disappeared for so long a time without checking with us to see if there are any new developments. If she tried some kind of heroics on her own, Coriander's people may have grabbed her, inside or outside the hotel."

"You know anything about Walter Ames's personal finances?" Hardy asked.

"Nothing for real," Chambrun said. "He lives expensively, according to Jim Priest. But he is a lobbyist for ITC—International Trade. That means he has contacts with big money all over the world."

"If Cleaves is dead broke and in trouble, as your man Andrews suggests," Hardy said, "his wife must know it. It would be logical for her to turn to her father."

"See if Ames has a telephone in Athens, New York," Chambrun said to me.

Information was very polite. Walter Ames did have a telephone, but it was unlisted and private. She couldn't give it out.

"I can handle that," Hardy said.

Five minutes later we had a number for Ames, but it rang and rang and nobody answered. I was ordered to keep trying, but as the evening wore on, Ames still didn't answer his phone and Connie remained among the missing.

TWO

OTHER THINGS HELPED to fill the evening. Valentine, the bomb squad man, turned up with an elderly gent named Crenshaw who turned out to be a member of the architectural firm that had designed and helped build the Beaumont. The original designer was long dead, but there were blueprints. Crenshaw was white-haired, jowly, with a red face and a heavily veined nose that suggested that his primary interest in life was alcohol. I could smell rye whiskey on his breath halfway across the room. But it didn't seem to affect his knowledge of the building. He gave us a brief lecture, using a silver pencil as a pointer to the blueprints which were spread out on Chambrun's desk.

"With explosives placed here, and here, and in these other places that Captain Valentine has described to me," he said, "I can tell you, Mr. Chambrun, that the damage would be staggering. Your Colonel Coriander exaggerates when he suggests the top ten floors of the hotel might come tumbling down, but he doesn't need that to happen for his threat to be very real."

"Let's have it," Chambrun said.

"To begin with," Crenshaw said, "a massive explosion in the elevator shaft would wreck that mechanism from top to bottom. It would take months to shore it up, rebuild it and make it operative. The rest of the charges, placed in the rooms on Fifteen and in the corridor would blow the entire floor into rubble, and probably do extensive damage on Fourteen and

Sixteen. I would have to advise you to have those two floors also evacuated."

Chambrun sat very still behind his desk, scowling. "Have you come up with any way to deactivate these explosives, Captain Valentine?" he asked.

"No way," Valentine said. "There is no way to get at the charges without Coriander being aware. We thought of trying to send men up the elevator shaft on the roof of a car and trying to remove the explosives in the shaft. But each one of these charges is wired to the next one. Start fiddling with any one of them and the man sitting at the detonator would know it. Unless you're prepared to give up on the hostages, we can't storm the fifteenth floor, and even if we tried, all that jerk at the detonator has to do is press a button and we'd all be blown to hell and gone. If Coriander's demands are met and he walks out of the hotel a free man—which will be one of his demands, of course—then we can reasonably be sure of deactivating the charges. He's got us by the short hairs, Mr. Chambrun."

"According to Captain Valentine the man at the detonator is in 1507," Crenshaw said, pointing to the blueprint with his pencil. "The windows to that room are on the east side—no ledge, of course, no outside fire escapes. I suppose it would be possible to lower a man, or men, down from one of the upper floors to those two windows in 1507. It would be touch and go then."

"Meaning?"

"Shoot the man at the detonator, smash in through the windows and disconnect the contraption before Coriander's army are aware of what's happening. Last

resort, I expect. I wouldn't like to try it, hanging in
space twelve hundred feet above the street.''

"The man at the detonator has a machine pistol
right on the table beside him," I said.

Crenshaw shrugged. "So you see—" he said.

So much for that kind of heroics.

Treadway, the Assistant Commissioner, had placed
himself in personal charge of the small army of policemen who were swarming over the Beaumont. They
were there to protect us from the rapidly growing army
of pickets outside all the entrances to the hotel, and
against any violence that might suddenly erupt inside. Inside, things went on as usual in the Trapeze
Bar, the Spartan Bar, and the Blue Lagoon Room,
which is a combination restaurant and night club. You
could sense a kind of special tension and excitement.
I sometimes wonder about people. I remember seeing
film clips of the shootout in California between the
cops and the Hearst kidnappers. Guns were being fired
like a full-scale war, but people were everywhere,
watching, risking death in order to be witnesses to a
blood-letting. You'd have imagined that people would
have stayed away from the Beaumont, being fully informed about the bomb threat. They didn't. They had
to be turned away from the Blue Lagoon, and they
were standing four deep at the bars. Violence seems to
be an unbelievable magnet.

I had a project of my own and Chambrun turned me
loose on it. I was concerned about the two little girls
and Katherine Horn held hostage on the fifteenth
floor; I was concerned about the threat to the hotel itself, not just the damage explosions might cause, but
what it might do to its future. Chambrun has said at
some time or other that the Beaumont is not just a

hotel, it's a way of life. That way of life might be dislocated for a long time by what was happening. But my concern was chiefly centered on Connie Cleaves. She had been gone for nearly ten hours without any word, without an inquiry from her about her children. It couldn't, it seemed to me, possibly be a voluntary disappearance. She was very real to me; the scent she wore, the touch of her hand, the brushing of her lips against my cheek, her momentary clinging to me in despair. I wanted to find her, and not for any of the lewd reasons that have been suggested. She was someone with big troubles who needed help. I wanted to give it to her if I could.

The one person who might be helpful since her father wasn't reachable seemed to me to be Colin Andrews, the newspaperman. He had been covering Cleaves for some time and he probably knew a great many intimate details about the entire family. There could be friends he would know of to whom Connie might have gone for help. Help meant money, huge sums of it. If she hadn't gone to her father, Andrews might know of someone else.

I had a feeling Andrews wouldn't be very far from the center of action and I wondered if he might actually have checked into the hotel. He hadn't, but after shouldering my way through a mob of people in the Trapeze Bar, I spotted him at a distant corner table. He was with a nice-looking blonde girl who turned out to be one of Cleaves's secretaries. He introduced me to Martha Blodgett.

Waiters were having difficulty serving the tables, the mob around the bar was so large and so noisy. You had to shout to carry on a conversation. I suggested the drinks would flow a little more freely and that we could hear ourselves think in my apartment. Andrews and Miss Blodgett seemed pleased to go there with me.

It wasn't until I had poured them drinks that I told them about my concern for Connie. I didn't tell them the Horween story. That was not yet for public consumption.

"It's hard to believe she would just take off," Martha Blodgett said. "Those kids mean everything to her. She's put up with hell in order to stay with them."

Andrews smiled at me, his eyes unblinking behind the tinted glasses. "You need a program to tell the players," he said. "Martha happens to be working my side of the street. She isn't fond of Terry Cleaves."

"But you work for him," I said.

"I work for Britain's U.N. staff," she said. "If Cleaves was removed tomorrow, I'd still be on the new ambassador's staff. I'm not English, you know. They need someone who knows New York and the American scene in general." She wrinkled her pretty nose. "Cleaves is a horse's derrière."

"It occurred to me that one of you might know where Connie can have gone," I said. "Someone to whom she might go for help?"

"And not inquire about her children for ten hours?" Andrews asked, frowning.

"Her father," Martha Blodgett said.

"We haven't been able to reach him."

"He has a sort of hideaway in a little town called Athens, in the Catskills," Martha said.

"We know, but we haven't been able to reach him there. He doesn't answer his phone."

"If anybody can raise the ransom money, it's Buck Ames," Andrews said.

"Connie'd know that," Martha said. "She'd also know that Cleaves doesn't have any chance at all of raising it personally. If she knew her father wasn't in Athens, but someplace some distance away, she may have gone to him."

"And still not checked back here to find out about the girls?"

"It's hard to imagine," Martha said.

"Neither of you has any other suggestion?" I asked.

I thought they exchanged a kind of uncertain glance. They knew something, I thought.

"Look here," I said. "I have two different stories, one from you, Andrews, and one from Jim Priest."

"Good man, Priest," Andrews said.

"He vouches for you," I said, "but he doubts your story, particularly one part of it. You tell me Cleaves is a woman chaser."

"My track shoes are worn out," Martha said.

"Priest tells me that the story is that Connie is the promiscuous sex addict in the family. Cleaves seems to back that up."

"There's always gossip about beautiful women," Martha said. "Unfortunately nobody gossips about me."

"I'd like the truth," I said. "Does Connie have a rich lover somewhere she can have gone to for help?"

"If she hasn't, she ought to have," Martha said.

"Why does she stay with Cleaves if he's what you say he is?" I asked.

"Because he's got something on her," Martha said.

"An affair or affairs?"

"He could take the children away from her if he has proof," Martha said.

Andrews lit a cigarette and sat staring at a small landscape by Eugene Ludins that hangs over one of the bookcases. "You're not out for something to pass on to the local gossip boys, are you, Haskell." It wasn't a question. It was a conclusion he'd come to. "Still, I can't tell you everything I know about Terrence Cleaves. Martha knows some of it; she's been digging for me on the inside. But if anything should leak, the sonofabitch might get off the hook before I can land him. I've been on his trail for two years, Haskell, and I can't risk having all that go down the drain."

"So you can't talk," I said. "All I want is help in finding Connie. Where she could have gone; if there is any other likely person beside her father she might count on for help. You must know the whole history of the Cleaves family, Colin. If there is someone like that—?" I let it lie there.

Colin Andrews took a deep drag on his cigarette. "So here is something," he said finally. "Until about four years ago the Cleaves marriage seemed to be a happy and successful one. It was about that time that Cleaves invested a very large sum of money, probably most of his liquid assets, into a project for manufacturing and marketing a new sports car."

"The T.C. 4," I said. "Priest told us that."

"It was a disaster," Andrews said. "The car was too expensive; inflation and taxes in Britain were eating up the average man alive. It was a question of coming up with a new product at the very worst possible time. Cleaves had to pour in more money to try to save his original investment. I know, from my research, that he mortgaged his property, borrowed, and—and eventually stole in an effort to save himself."

"Stole?"

"Used funds that didn't belong to him," Andrews said. "Then he was faced with finding money to replace what he had stolen. Most of his friends had no idea how bad his situation was. They knew he'd taken a whipping, but not how bad a whipping. All this time he was in highly sensitive positions in the government. He knew things about international financial dealings in which our government was involved. And he knew a great deal about our defense plans, our secret diplomacy. In short he was a man in a position of the highest trust. He still is, or he wouldn't be at the United Nations. But we live in a time when political leaks are part of the world of government. You people in this country know how it was with Watergate. A whiff of smoke here, another there, suggesting a raging fire somewhere. Some of those whiffs of smoke came my way, which is when I started to work on the Cleaves story. What those whiffs were are what I can't talk about, Mark, beyond saying that Cleaves found enough money to save himself from a public bankruptcy and a scandal. Where it came from is what concerns me. I think I can tell you that I'm certain he sold information which came his way as a trusted public servant to foreign interests. I think, in short, he is guilty of treason. I don't yet have the proof that would hang him."

"Connie is my concern," I reminded him.

"It was in this time when he had to cover up a theft or be exposed that the marriage fell apart," Andrews said. "My guess is that Cleaves went to Buck Ames and was turned down flat. The old buccaneer had always been openly unfriendly to his son-in-law. I don't know the reasons for that, except that Ames is a man of passionate likes and dislikes, passionate pleasures, passionate grudges and animosities. Cleaves was on his enemy list, and I think he refused flatly to help, even to save Connie from going down with the ship. It was after that Cleaves began, discreetly enough as far as the public was concerned, to enjoy the company of other women, all kinds of women. I know for certain that he flaunted them in front of Connie. He actually brought them home to his own house and made love to them with Connie and the children there on another floor."

"And Connie put up with it?" I asked, hardly believing.

"She put up with it for a long time," Andrews said. He was frowning at the ash on his cigarette. "I got to talk to a maid in the household who left because Cleaves found her conveniently attractive. She didn't understand why or how Connie could take it. She did tell me that she overheard a breakfast table conversation at which Connie protested on account of the children and Cleaves told her she would damn well take it and like it or she knew what he would do to her."

"What?" I asked.

"I don't know," Andrews said. "But he has some hold on her that is something a good deal more than custody of the children. And at that time, Mark, take notice that there wasn't the slightest hint from any source that Connie was anything but a faithful and dutiful wife."

"At that time? So there was a later time?"

Andrews nodded slowly. "How much can a woman take, laughed at, degraded in front of a collection of cheap trollops? There was a man, an attractive young fellow in the Foreign Secretary's office. He'd come to parties at the Cleaves house in the days before all these horrors started. Connie ran into him somewhere, broke down and told him her troubles, and needing love and sympathy, wound up in his bed. For some reason Cleaves must have had his wife watched. He broke into the young man's house, gave him an unmerciful beating that hospitalized him for months, and dragged Connie, wrapped only in a sheet, out onto the street and into his car. Right after that Connie began to be seen everywhere with a collection of men, different ones every night, making something of a public display of herself.'' Andrews put out his cigarette. ''I dug into this as far as I could, Mark, and I came to the conclusion that this was all window dressing. I couldn't find a shred of evidence that she was ever seriously involved with any of these men. The gossip Priest reported to you was very real. But I'd bet my last shilling that Connie was putting on a show and not sleeping with half the young males in London.''

''Why would she put on such a show?'' Martha asked.

''Punishment,'' Andrews said. ''When an attractive woman like Connie belongs to a man and starts running around in public with dozens of others—'' He shrugged. ''People certainly must have wondered what was wrong with Cleaves. Great athlete, national hero, why couldn't he satisfy his wife?''

''But none of these boyfriends come to mind as someone she might turn to in trouble? What about the first one, the one Cleaves clobbered?'' I asked.

''Poor fellow got one of the ghastly far-out assignments in the Foreign Service—Burma, Pakistan, God knows where," Andrews said. "No, Connie can't have gone to him, even if she knows where he is."

My phone rang and I went over to the center table to answer. I glanced at my watch as I picked up the instrument. It was going on one o'clock in the morning. It was Chambrun on the phone.

"I just had a call from Walter Ames," he said.

"Connie's with him?" I asked, feeling relieved.

"No," Chambrun said. "He called, asking for her. Been on some kind of a boat cruise up the Hudson. No radio or TV. He hadn't heard the news until he got home a short time ago. He's on his way. Should arrive in about an hour."

"He can't drive a hundred and twenty-five miles in an hour, even at night," I said.

"Helicopter," Chambrun said. "Buck Ames always does things in style. You've had no luck?"

"Nothing practical. Some gossip."

"Well, if you can stay awake till Ames arrives—"

BUCK AMES was like a blast of fresh wind as he came charging into Chambrun's office about two o'clock that morning. I was instantly reminded of the present-day Caesar Romero, the movie actor—a big man, white-haired, with a beak of a nose over a black mustache and white-toothed smile. Black eyebrows shaded very bright black eyes. He was suntanned to a mahogany brown, and though I suspect he was sixty years old, he looked trim and well-muscled as an exercised man of thirty. Something in the shape of his face was reminiscent of the more delicate, fine-boned Connie. His voice was big, booming—the Buccaneer shouting his commands from the quarter-deck. He ignored me as if I was a useless piece of furniture and bore down on Chambrun.

"You're Chambrun," he said. "Have you found Connie?"

Chambrun shook his head.

"Jesus H. Christ, why not?" Buck shouted. "You've got the whole goddam city police force, the FBI, your own security people. Why not?"

"Because we're walking on eggs in this case, Mr. Ames," Chambrun said. "I'd like you to know Mark Haskell, a trusted assistant. He's been looking for Connie."

"Without any luck," I said.

"I'll lay ten to one I can tell you where she is," Buck said.

"We hoped you could," Chambrun said. "That's why we've been trying to reach you all night."

"She's upstairs on the fifteenth floor with those crazy bastards," Buck said. "She'd want to be with her kids. She's given herself up as another hostage."

"I thought of that," Chambrun said quietly. "But I've had to write it off."

"Why?" Buck demanded. "I know that girl like I know myself. Nothing would keep her away from those kids. She knows how scared they must be. She knows how badly they must need her."

He was right, of course. I wondered why I hadn't thought of that myself. And as I wondered, Chambrun knocked it down.

"Pour Mr. Ames a drink of whatever he wants, Mark," he said. "And help yourself."

"Bourbon, neat, and don't spare the horses," Buck said, before I could ask him. "Why did you write off that theory, Chambrun?"

"I told you, we're walking on eggs, Mr. Ames."

"Buck, for Christ sake," Buck said. "Everybody calls me Buck including my no-good son-in-law."

"I wrote it off, Buck, because there's no way she could have got there or made contact with this Coriander fellow without my knowing," Chambrun said. "The phones to the fifteenth floor are open. We don't interfere with calls in or out, but we monitor them. Your daughter hasn't made any attempt to contact Coriander by phone, nor has he made any attempt to reach her. There is no way to get to the fifteenth floor without having to pass one of our security guards on the stairway or in an elevator. No one she would have to pass to get there has seen her."

"Someone slipped up, took a walk, went to the john."

"My people are working in pairs in that area," Chambrun said.

"So you and the government and the cops and the FBI are just sitting around on your ass doing nothing and waiting for Coriander to call the tune, right?"

"Your son-in-law is trying to raise the ransom money," Chambrun said.

"Don't make me laugh!" Buck said, and actually roared with laughter. "He couldn't raise the money to buy the dog tag his late mother should be wearing. Raise the ransom! If that's the kind of thinking that's going on around here, God help us! Look, Chambrun, I haven't heard anything but the reports on the radio in my helicopter. Bring me up to date."

Chambrun spun it out for him and to my surprise added the Horween story to it.

"I know Doug Horween," Buck said. "He's just the kind of reckless bastard who'd try that sort of thing. You buy it? You think they killed him?"

"Horween had a rare blood type—AB negative. The police phoned me a few minutes ago to tell me the bloodstains on the clothes match. AB negative."

That was news I hadn't had till then.

"Horween has walked a tightrope all his life over a cage full of hungry lions," Buck said. "Sooner or later he was bound to fall in. He always took too big chances. That's why the limeys fired him out of their spy service, or whatever it's called." He tossed down the old-fashioned glass full of bourbon I brought him as though it was water. "My horse's ass son-in-law took him in because he's the same kind of reckless gambler, without the same kind of iron in his system. I'm sorry about Horween. He was an interesting character. Too bad it couldn't have been Terry boy."

"We've been presented with a theory about Terrence Cleaves," Chambrun said quietly.

"I don't need theories about him. I know about him, all about him," Buck said. "Someday, when I have nothing left to live for, I'm going to take pleasure in disemboweling him."

"Why does Connie stay with him?" I asked.

"Because she's an idiot, God love her. Because she loves him in spite of everything."

"I don't believe that," I said.

Buck's black eyes burned into me. "Has she been playing her game of musical beds with you?" he asked.

"I don't think she plays musical beds," I said.

"Ah! Love raises its ugly head."

"Don't be absurd. I scarcely know her. But a man who does, tells me there's nothing to that rumor."

"So you found one who doesn't kiss and tell," Buck said.

"I found a man named Andrews who has a special interest in your son-in-law," I said.

The black eyebrows rose. "Colin Andrews—*London Times*?"

"The same. I just left him fifteen minutes ago."

"It's Andrews who presented us with a theory," Chambrun said. "He thinks Cleaves may actually be Coriander. That this whole thing is a scheme for him to raise money for himself. That the political demands are just diversionary."

Buck's red lips pursed in a long, low whistle. "Sweet Judas," he said. "That's just the kind of scheme Terry boy might dream up. What have you done about it?"

"Nothing except launch inquiries," Chambrun said. "There's nothing we can do. Mark has been upstairs. He's seen the layout, the guns, the ammunition, the explosives. Coriander, whoever he is, isn't bluffing."

Buck turned to me and a nerve twitched at the corner of his mouth. "You saw the children?"

"Saw them, talked to them. They were holding up well. That was a long time ago, late yesterday morning. Miss Horn, the governess, is with them."

"That bitch is one of Terry boy's girl friends," Buck said. "She'd know if this was a scheme of his."

"And you think it may be?" Chambrun asked.

Buck handed me his empty glass without looking at me. I took it over to the sideboard and refilled it. His dark brows were drawn together in a scowl. "I've got such a strong bias," he said. "Anything bad anyone told me about Terrence Cleaves I'd believe. But I also know men."

"Meaning?"

"Cleaves is a stupid villain," Buck said. "He has no conscience, no morals, but I'd have said he wasn't bright enough to think up a scheme like this. He's a hit-and-run kind of a jerk. This Coriander, whoever he is, is a real cool operator. He's willing to sit up there for days, with a whole army camped around him, waiting to get exactly what he wants. Terry boy hasn't the constitution to sweat out anything like that. Thirty men up there, you say. He couldn't get thirty men to go along with him on any project. Of course—" Buck's voice trailed off.

"Yes?"

"Coriander could have included Terry in," Buck said. "Terry could be working on the outside for him, promised a piece of the pie."

"He'd let them use his own children?" I asked.

"He'd send those kids to the sausage factory if it would suit his purposes," Buck said. He squared his shoulders and tossed off his second drink. "Well, I'm not going to sit here and let them play games with those kids and Connie. Because I still think she got up there somehow."

"What do you propose doing?" Chambrun asked very quietly.

"I'm going to find the money," Buck said, his voice harsh. "I'm going to offer it for the return of the kids and Connie. Then, if Coriander turns me down, I'll know he has no intention of ever letting them go. They can identify him by now, you know. He can't wear that false face all the time. I promise you one thing, Chambrun. He isn't going to get away with this, if I have to blow up your goddam hotel with him in it to get him!''

Chambrun smiled, his sphinxlike smile. ''Well, getting the money should keep you busy for a while, Buck.''

Buck looked dead serious. ''You know what my job is, Chambrun? I work for ITC, biggest of all the multi-national corporations. You think we don't have an army of our own? That's how you fight an army— with an army. If anything happens to those kids and Connie, I'll wipe this Army For Justice off the face of the earth and Coriander will be buried at the bottom of your elevator shaft.''

We watched him storm out of the office. I was too tired from the long, tense day to try to figure out whether he was for real or not. I remember walking over to the sideboard to pour myself a drink. My legs felt a little wobbly under me. Chambrun, one of his Egyptian cigarettes balanced between stubby fingers, was watching me. He looked as fresh as if he'd just gotten up from a good night's sleep instead of having been on the job, nonstop, for about eighteen hours.

''You better get some rest,'' he said to me. ''This is going to get down to the nitty-gritty in a few hours. There are going to be some answers for Coriander that he won't like.''

''You've had some word?'' I asked.

''Let's face it,'' he said. ''Nobody is going to consider for a minute releasing those prisoners in Vietnam. And the Pentagon isn't going to send its generals to jail. The money may be found, but that's all.''

''If Andrews is right, the money is all that's important,'' I said.

"Could be," Chambrun said, sinking back into some private thoughts. "Get some rest."

I went down the hall to my apartment. The area was deserted now. The people who had crowded there earlier in the day were gone, and the security people were now at the bottom of the stairway and the elevator bank to keep anyone from getting up. The bars and the Blue Lagoon would be closed now and the Beaumont had settled down to something like normal, even with the explosive danger ever present on the fifteenth floor.

I walked like a man in a trance to the apartment and opened the door with my key. I switched on the lights.

I stood there with my mouth hanging open. Someone had ripped the place to pieces. Books had been thrown out of the cases, cushions on the couch and in the chairs tossed around. My desk had been searched, drawers open, papers strewn around. I couldn't believe it. I didn't keep anything here that was of any real value to anyone, except possibly the few small paintings I've mentioned. They'd been taken off the wall, evidently to search their backs for something.

I wondered about the rest of the apartment and I moved unsteadily toward the bedroom. Even before I reached it, I could feel the small hairs rising on the back of my neck. There was the faint scent of a perfume I remembered. As I reached the door, a voice spoke out of the darkness—a small, broken voice.

"Please—please don't turn on the light, Mark."

"For God sake, Connie!" I said. I could see the outline of her body stretched out on my bed, arms thrown up over her face.

"Please!" she said. "Not the light."

I stepped into the bathroom and turned on the light
there. It provided enough to see her clearly without
providing any glare. I went over to the bed and sat
down beside her. She turned away, moaning slightly.

"Where have you been?" I asked. "We've been
crazy with anxiety for you. What's happened?"

"Oh, my God," she whispered.

I told hold of her hands. They were cold as ice. I
pulled them gently away from her face. Suddenly she
turned onto her back and looked up at me.

"Oh, Jesus!" I heard myself say.

I say she looked up at me, but that's just a figure of
speech. Her eyes were swollen and almost closed. Her
whole face was dark with swellings and bruises. There
was a little trickle of blood at one corner of her
mouth.

She had taken a brutal beating from someone, almost beyond description.

THREE

I REACHED FOR THE bedside phone and called Dr. Partridge, the house physician. He's a crotchety old bird and responded to my summons with a string of profanity that wasn't designed for delicate ears. He is always outraged if anyone needs his help after he's gone to bed, or during one of his endless games of backgammon in the Spartan Bar.

All the time I talked to him Connie kept clutching at me and saying, "No—no, Mark—please, no!"

Then I called Chambrun and gave him a quick one-two.

"Don't touch anything in your living room," was all he said.

Then Connie was clinging to me, sobbing.

"What in God's name happened to you?" I asked her. "Who did this to you?"

She turned her head from side to side. I thought she couldn't answer because of the tears. I disentangled myself and went out into the living room and fixed the door latch so that Chambrun and Doc Partridge could get in. Then I poured a jigger of brandy for Connie and took it back into the bedroom. She protested at first, but then she drank it, choking a little after she tossed it off in one gulp. Then Chambrun was standing beside us.

"How long have you been here, Mrs. Cleaves?" he asked.

"Just—just a few minutes," she said.

"Was Mark's place torn apart the way it is when you came?"

"Yes."

"Do you know who did it?"

"No." She was hanging onto me again, her fingernails biting into my arms.

"But you certainly know who beat you up."

She didn't answer, but buried her face against my shoulder.

"You've been gone since early afternoon, Mrs. Cleaves," Chambrun said. "Where have you been?"

No answer. And then old Doc Partridge, wearing an ancient flannel bathrobe and carrying his black bag, joined us. He took one look at Connie and began to swear under his breath again.

"Get the hell out of my way," he said to me, "and turn on a light. I can't do a damn thing in the dark."

With the light on she looked worse than I'd thought. The skin was broken over one cheekbone. Her swollen eyes were a dark purple. Her jaw, somehow, looked a little lopsided.

"This didn't happen five minutes ago," Doc Partridge said. "When and who did it, girl?"

Chambrun's voice was cold and without sympathy. "A family quarrel?" he asked.

Connie winced as Doc Partridge swabbed at the cut cheekbone with cotton dipped in something from his bag.

"You got a husband who did this, girl?" Doc asked as he worked. "Sonofabitch ought to be in jail. You bring charges against him, hear me?" He looked up at Chambrun. "I don't think the jaw is broken, but it could be. I suggest the hospital."

"No!" Connie cried out.

"Mrs. Cleaves is the mother of the two children who are being held up on Fifteen," Chambrun told Doc.

We had another customer then. Jerry Dodd came in, obviously sent for by Chambrun after I'd called.

"There must be some fingerprints in that mess out there," Chambrun said, gesturing toward the living room. Jerry ducked back out there and Chambrun picked up the bedside phone. He got the night supervisor. "Mrs. Kiley? Terrence Cleaves has been assigned a room while Fifteen is out of business. Room 805, I think. Connect me." He waited, frowning down at Connie. Then: "Cleaves? Pierre Chambrun here. Your wife has had an accident. She's in Mark Haskell's apartment on the second floor." Pause. "Well, you damn well better make it your business or I'll send the police to pick you up." He slammed down the receiver. "Have you been with your husband all afternoon and evening?" he asked Connie.

Again her head turned from side to side. "Please, I've got nothing to tell you, Mr. Chambrun. It's—it's a private matter."

"Do you know that your father is in town looking for you?"

"Oh, God," she said. "Does he—does he have to know?"

"He has to know, Mrs. Cleaves, and I have to know," Chambrun said.

He didn't wait for her to tell him, however. He turned toward the living room, gesturing for me to follow. We joined Jerry Dodd out there and Chambrun closed the bedroom door. Jerry was dusting the desk for fingerprints.

"Place is lousy with fingerprints," Jerry said. "You had an army in here, Mark?"

There was me, of course, and Connie, and there had been Colin Andrews and Martha Blodgett for a drink earlier on.

"I'm playing a hunch," Chambrun said. "Terrence Cleaves should show up here in a minute or two, Jerry. The minute he does, head up to 805 and get a sample of his prints. I'm guessing you'll find it matched somewhere in this room."

Jerry nodded and went on with his work.

"How did Mrs. Cleaves get in here?" Chambrun asked.

"No sweat. I gave her a key when I first brought her here."

"So Cleaves beat her up, took the key from her, and came here to look for what, Mark?"

"Search me."

"She didn't give you anything to keep for her?"

"No."

"Cleaves had to believe she'd left something here that was important to him," Chambrun said. "Something she'd try to hide; otherwise, why the books, the paintings?"

Jerry was photographing prints with a tiny pocket camera when there was a sharp knock at the door. I opened it and Terrence Cleaves was standing outside, tall and straight, his eyes blazing with anger. He brushed past me and walked straight up to Chambrun, towering over him.

"I resent your ordering me about, Chambrun," he said. "As for the police, you very well know that I enjoy diplomatic immunity. What is this about an accident to Constance?"

"Figure of speech," Chambrun said. "There was nothing accidental about the beating you gave her."

"What the hell are you talking about?" Cleaves demanded.

Chambrun turned away from him, went to the bedroom door and opened it. He stood aside for Cleaves to go by him. At the sight of her husband Connie turned her face away from Doc Partridge's ministrations. The old doctor looked around.

"This the husband?" he asked. His eyes glittered. "I'll tell you something, fella. You ought to have your ass kicked around the block and I'd be glad to join in the fun. This girl is hurt."

Cleaves's face was rock-hard. His eyes remained fixed on Connie. "Does she say I did this to her?" he asked.

"She doesn't say anything," Doc Partridge said. "You may have broken her jaw."

Cleaves did an about-face like a soldier on parade and stalked out into the living room. Chambrun closed the bedroom door.

"You'll see to it that she gets the best of care," Cleaves said.

I noticed that Jerry Dodd was gone.

"Aren't you curious about what's happened in this room?" Chambrun asked.

"There's only one thing in the whole damn world I'm interested in," Cleaves said, his voice harsh. "That's finding the money that may ransom my children. Is there any news from upstairs?"

"I suppose the legal position is that if your wife won't bring charges against you you can beat her to your heart's content," Chambrun said. "But breaking into this room and tearing it apart is another story."

"That's an absurd suggestion," Cleaves said. "In any event I have diplomatic immunity."

"Did you know that Buck Ames is in town?" Chambrun asked.

Cleaves turned sharply. "When? Where is he?"

"I have the feeling that when he gets a look at Connie, diplomatic immunity isn't going to do you much good, Mr. Cleaves," Chambrun said.

"Then for God's sake let her accuse me!" Cleaves almost shouted.

"Her silence is an accusation," Chambrun said. "What did she have that you wanted so badly?"

"I've had enough of this," Cleaves said, and started for the door.

Before he reached it, it opened and Jerry Dodd came in. He closed the door and stood with his back to it. "His prints are all over Mark's desk," he said.

Cleaves's handsome face turned a sickly gray. You could almost hear his mind working. He was wondering if he could charge past Jerry and get away. Jerry, who was four inches shorter and forty pounds lighter, looked almost hungry for it to happen. I'd seen Jerry handle big men who got obstreperous. It was rather pretty to watch.

Cleaves took a handkerchief out of his pocket and blotted at a trickle of sweat that had started to run down his cheek. He'd evidently decided against trying to tackle Jerry. Perhaps he'd guessed it would be as unequal as it looked.

"So you did rip this room apart," Chambrun said in his prosecutor's voice.

Cleaves's broad shoulders drooped. "She had something of importance that belongs to me," he said, his voice low. "She refused to tell me where she'd hidden it."

"So you beat her up, and when that didn't work, you came down here to find it," Chambrun said.

"She was trying to blackmail me with it," Cleaves said. "It is something important to my job, my position of trust, my country."

"There are indications in 805," Jerry Dodd said casually, "that she may have been tied up there in an armchair. Some strips of adhesive tape that got thrown in the wastebasket, a bathrobe cord. I think she managed to get away while he was gone somewhere, and came back here."

"Or did he bring her down here and try to get her to show him where she'd hidden whatever it is he wanted? Maybe some of the beating took place here," Chambrun suggested. "What was she blackmailing you for, Cleaves? What did she want from you?"

Cleaves moistened his lips. They looked blue. "The children," he said. "Custody of the children."

"Need I point out that Coriander has custody of the children?" Chambrun asked.

"After—after they're free," Cleaves said.

"What you were looking for is a document of some kind? A letter, perhaps?" Chambrun asked.

Cleaves seemed to have turned to stone. He didn't answer.

"How much chance do you think you have of raising the ransom money?" Chambrun asked.

Cleaves shrugged. "Unless the governments will help—"

"Can Buck Ames raise it?"

"It's not impossible," Cleaves said.

Chambrun took a cigarette out of his silver case and lit it.

"Can he get away with this?" I asked, gesturing around the room.

"There's one thing Mr. Terrence Cleaves can't do," Chambrun said. "He can't hide. The whole world is watching him, waiting to see what happens on the fifteenth floor. I think it will be up to the lady to decide what's to be done about this. Let me warn you, Cleaves. The heat is going to begin to get hot in the morning. Coriander will begin to be impatient, I feel certain. Maybe you should go to Buck Ames for help."

"Joke!" Cleaves said bitterly.

"Let him go, Jerry," Chambrun said.

"You're kidding," Jerry said, looking disappointed.

"For now," Chambrun said.

Jerry stood aside, and the Coldstream Guardsman walked, stiff and straight, out of the room. At the same moment Doc Partridge appeared in the bedroom doorway, snapping closed his black bag.

"She'll do," he said. "Only time is going to heal those bruises. I left her some medication to help." He looked around. "You let the husband go?"

"We gave him a little rope," Chambrun said. "Jerry, I want Cleaves followed every minute, inside and outside the hotel. I want to be able to put my hand on his shoulder any time I need him."

"Right," Jerry said, and was gone.

Chambrun turned to me. "You may seem less like a policeman to Mrs. Cleaves than anyone else, Mark. Maybe she'll come clean with you. It's worth a try. Keep in touch."

So I was alone in my wrecked apartment, with Connie in the next room. It wasn't exactly how I'd imagined it might be.

SHE LAY ON HER BACK on the bed. She was fully dressed, of course, but Doc Partridge had pulled a sheet up over her and supplied her with two gauze patches, soaked in something, that rested over her eyes. She was breathing slowly, regularly. I thought she might be asleep, that exhaustion had overtaken her. But when I reached down and touched her hand, her fingers closed tightly around mine.

I sat down on the edge of the bed.

"Have they gone?" she whispered.

"Gone," I said. "Can I get you anything? Another drink?"

"Was it brandy I had before?"

I went into the next room and brought back the bottle of Cognac and a glass. I poured a little for her, and this time she sipped it the way brandy should be drunk. I took the glass from her hands and put it on the bedside table.

"We have a pretty clear picture of some of it," I said. "It was Cleaves who wrecked the other room. Fingerprints. Our security man thinks he had you tied up in 805. Have you been there all the time since you left here?"

"Till he brought me back here," she said. I had to lean close to her to hear her.

"To find the document or the letter you'd taken from him?" I asked.

"He told you I had something of his?"

"Yes."

"That's not so," she said. "Not true. I have something he wanted, but it's not his."

"What?"

Her scarlet mouth quivered slightly. "The truth about him," she said.

"Care to tell me?"

"No, Mark, I can't tell you."

"Will you bring charges against him for what he did to you?"

"No."

"I don't understand," I said.

Her hand tightened on mine. "I had what may seem to you to have been a mad idea," she said. "I intended to call this Coriander man and ask him to let me be with the girls; to hold me as a hostage, too."

"Chambrun thought that might be where you were, but we knew you hadn't contacted Coriander and that you couldn't have gone up to Fifteen without being seen by our security people."

"I had to see Terrence first before I tried it," she said.

"Oh?"

"I had to be sure that he'd do everything in his power to meet Coriander's demands."

"And you didn't think he would?"

"I thought he'd fail as far as the money's concerned and that he'd give up. He'd leave it to someone else who had nothing at stake."

"Your father. He cares. He's trying now to find the money."

"Poor dear Buck," she said. "He'll find that it's easy to raise money for oil wells, for steel mills, for airplanes, but not for two little girls. There's no return on that kind of money; no interest, no profits, no capital gains. He'll try, I know. But there had to be someone who could be *made* to make it work.''

"So you have something on your husband?"

She nodded slowly. "I have facts about him that could smash him forever," she said. "I sat down at your desk and I wrote down where the proofs could be found. I sent them, with a note, to a friend of mine. If anything happens to me, she is to pass the letter on to someone who will know how to use the information."

I took a long shot. "Colin Andrews?" I asked.

She turned her head. "You know Colin?"

"I know him, and what he believes about your husband."

"He's right. Well, I told Terrence what I'd done. Not who I'd sent the letter to, of course. He thought— he thought I might have given it to you. He tried to make me tell him." She lifted fingertips to her bruised face.

"So get to your friend and tell her to turn the information over to Andrews," I said.

"No."

"Why the hell not?"

"It must be the last thing, the last act. When everything else has failed, not before. Terrence knows now that he must pull out all the stops. If by some miracle he succeeds, then I keep his secret. Don't worry about me, Mark. He won't try anything more to hurt me. He won't dare."

It was quite clear she wasn't going to tell me any more. I poured a little more brandy for her and held it to her lips.

"Don't leave me alone, Mark," she said.

I stretched out on the bed beside her and put an arm around her. She drew a deep breath and was asleep before I could say another word to her.

IT WAS A STRANGE INTERLUDE in a time of violence. I lay still beside her, holding her gently. In her sleep she pressed her body against mine and her coppery hair was next to my face. I cared about her, I thought; I cared about what happened to her; I felt a fierce anger against the man who had beaten her; I puzzled over why she didn't let him have both barrels. I didn't quite understand her explanation. It didn't matter. She had asked me to stay with her, to be her protector. I guess, eventually, I dozed off, not wanting to move my arm, which was cramped and uncomfortable, for fear it would disturb her.

Would you believe that I had almost literally forgotten the one-armed man in 15 A? I'd forgotten the murder of Horween, and the two little girls who must now be frozen with fear since no one seemed to be doing anything to get them released. I had forgotten that with every beat of Connie's heart, which I could feel against my chest, time was running out for those children. Inside and outside the hotel Coriander's Army For Justice must be preparing for the next move. They wouldn't wait, motionless and inactive, forever. A little girl's ear, a hand, a foot! Would you believe I had wiped all that out of my consciousness as I cruised in and out of sleep, holding another man's wife, and imagining some future time when it would make more sense?

I MIGHT BE standing still in space, but not the rest of the world. Everywhere presses were rolling with the full story of the kidnapping and Coriander's demands. Men on trucks were tossing bundled accounts of the situation to corner newsdealers and in front of small stores for the early morning readers. I need only to have pressed a button to discover that all-night talk shows on television had been with the story, hour after hour. Diplomats and government heads in Europe, five hours ahead of us and well into their day, had opinions that were being expressed. England in particular was being very vocal, since the victims of Coriander's scheme were British subjects. Official comments were guarded. Only the United States government could do anything about political prisoners in Vietnam. Unofficial voices were more positive. The United States had turned a blind eye to the actions of the South Vietnamese government, her ally in Indochina. Now the day of reckoning was at hand.

Crackpots everywhere had opinions. We were reminded that the "tiger cages" in which political prisoners were held in Vietnam had been supplied by Uncle Sam, actually manufactured in this country. Isolated groups of veterans of the war in Vietnam applauded Coriander. It was time attention was called to the duplicity of the Peace With Honor. It was time the real villains in the world of the Pentagon were forced to face up to some kind of real justice. Harley Latham, that ever-present man of God, publicly prayed for the cleansing of our national conscience. "No price is too high to pay for the safety of two innocent children!" he told the all-night audiences. "They are worth more than all the armies, all the power, all the men in high places." He would personally urge the President, he promised, to pay whatever the price might be for the release of those innocent children, and he was certain every mother in the United States would support his plea.

Outside the Beaumont the army of pickets, augmented by hundreds of uninvolved curiosity hounds, grew to such proportions that the police were forced to reroute traffic around four blocks of Fifth Avenue. Across the street in Central Park people brought blankets and their breakfasts and lunches, prepared to make the death watch a kind of national picnic.

For real, a grim-faced James Priest, State Department, discussed the facts of life with Chambrun, the Assistant Police Commissioner, a representative of the mayor's office, Captain Valentine of the bomb squad, Gus Brand of the FBI, Lieutenant Hardy of Homicide, and hotel security represented by Jerry Dodd, as dawn crept over the city.

The President would make a public announcement at nine in the morning that the government was considering the possibility of meeting Coriander's demands. He would say that the Pentagon was reexamining the possible guilt of higher-ups. But, Priest told his audience, this simply represented the willingness of the President to stall for a little time. Political prisoners could not be released. No way. Even if the Pentagon was honestly reexamining, it would take months to bring new men to trial.

Priest was asked about the money.

"It would take an act of Congress for the government to give away such a huge sum," Priest said. "The congressmen would have to get what they call 'the sense of their constituents.' Most Americans will have a deep sympathy for the little girls, but those same Americans in very large numbers will oppose the idea that the government of the United States submit to blackmail by a criminal. You've seen that attitude in a jail in Texas where innocent hostages were shot rather than submit to blackmail by the criminals; you saw it at Attica; people on hijacked planes are regretfully abandoned by the authorities; there is a long history of refusing to be intimidated.''

"So we stall, with phony promises, while pieces of little girls are sent back to us on their breakfast trays," Chambrun said.

"Until you find a way to storm the fifteenth floor," Priest said.

"And have the hostages and ourselves blown to pieces," Chambrun said.

"Coriander might settle for the money and a safe way to escape," Gus Brand said. "He must know the other demands can't and won't be met."

"I have never thought anything but the money mattered," Chambrun said. "The other demands simply make it all seem more righteous to some people. Let's suppose the money can be found. How do we assure the escape of thirty people? I know your system, Mr. Brand. You'll have a hundred sharpshooters ready to mow them down the minute they leave the fifteenth floor. They'll have the hostages with them, because of course no one will be released until they're safely away. So everyone dies and we save the money. That's an American 'attitude' too, isn't it?''

Gus Brand didn't answer.

"There has to be a way," Jim Priest said.

"I'm willing to listen," Chambrun said. "I've spent the last twenty hours trying to think of a way and I've come up empty."

While all this was going on, I drowsed through the first light of morning, holding Connie in my arms.

The telephone bell in my living room sounded shrill and harsh. I came awake, and Connie stirred and moaned softly in her sleep. I managed to stumble up and go into the living room to answer the persistent ringing.

An anguished woman's voice that I didn't recognize in my foggy state said, "For God's sake help me, Mark!"

"Who is this?"

"Martha. Martha Blodgett."

"What's wrong? Where are you?"

"They assigned me a room on the tenth floor," she said, her voice breaking. "Ten fourteen." All of Cleaves's staff had been on Fifteen and were now scattered around the hotel.

"What's wrong?" I said again.

"Please come, Mark. Please!"

"Look, I've got trouble here," I said. "I'll send someone if you're in real trouble. I—"

"It's Colin!" she cried out. "They've killed him, Mark."

"What are you saying?" I must have sounded like a dummy to her.

"Oh, my God, will you please come!" she said.

"Hang up," I said. "I'm bringing help."

I called the switchboard and asked them to locate Jerry Dodd. I was told he was in Chambrun's office. I got Chambrun and told him what Martha had just said. When I met him out in the hall, having left Connie still asleep, not only was Jerry with him but also Lieutenant Hardy, the homicide man.

"No more details than you gave me?" Chambrun asked as we waited for an elevator.

"'They've killed him' is all she said."

I guess we reached 1014 within five minutes of Martha Blodgett's call. She answered our knock the instant Jerry's knuckles rapped on the door. She was wearing a pale blue robe. A river of blood was running down from her disheveled blond hair across her face and down onto the robe which she clutched around her throat. She didn't speak, but just stood aside to let us in.

I know I turned away because I thought I was going to be sick at my stomach. What may have been Colin Andrews lay twisted on the bed, stark naked, his head battered in like a smashed pumpkin. The sheets and the pillows looked as if they'd been used to mop up a slaughterhouse.

FOUR

THE FIRST THING TO DO was get Martha away from there and leave the bloody arena to Hardy and his homicide squad, who would presently be riding sirens through the city streets. We were clumsy about it, I suppose. Martha was barefooted, and she obviously had nothing on under her bloodstained blue robe. Like other people who had been shut off the fifteenth floor by Coriander, she had almost no personal belongings. An empty box from the lobby boutique suggested the robe was something she'd bought there since yesterday morning, along with an inexpensive comb and brush on the bureau. The dress she'd been wearing when she and Colin Andrews had been in my apartment was on a hangar in the closet. A pair of panty hose and a bra were on another hangar. Shoes neatly placed in the middle of the otherwise empty closet.

Colin Andrews' clothes were draped over an armchair.

"Bring Miss Blodgett's things, Mark. My office," Chambrun said. There was no other place to take her.

Hardy held up the exodus for a moment. "A brief statement, please, Miss Blodgett. You saw who did it?"

"No." A whisper.

It was awkward. She and Andrews had obviously been in bed together, and probably not to sleep. Martha was standing by me and she reached out to my arm to steady herself. It took guts for her to go on.

"We were making love," she said almost inaudibly. "Someone struck Colin and he—he rolled away from me, trying to escape, I think. And then I was struck." She lifted her hand to her bloodied hair. "That was all. I didn't see anyone. I—I must have been unconscious for a while. I don't know how long. What time is it?"

"Five-thirty," Hardy said.

"A half hour, then," Martha said. "When I came to I—oh, my God—I saw Colin like that—the way he is. I called Mark, the only person I could think of to call."

"You heard whoever it was come into the room?"

"No." She fought encroaching tears. "We were making sounds together—loving sounds. Can you understand, Lieutenant? I wasn't listening for anything."

"The door wasn't forced," Jerry Dodd said. "Whoever it was had a key. Coming could have been almost noiseless."

"Has anything been taken from your room?" Hardy asked.

"There was nothing to take, Lieutenant. I had nothing here except this robe I bought, a comb and brush, a toothbrush and paste in the bathroom. Everything I own is upstairs in the room I had on Fifteen."

"Handbag?"

"There on the bureau."

"May I look at the contents, Miss Blodgett?"

"Yes. There's nothing in it—a lipstick, an American Express credit card, some tissues, about six dollars in bills and some change, the door keys to this room and my room on Fifteen.''

Hardy opened the bag and looked at what he held. ''Nothing missing,'' he said.

''Can't this wait, Hardy, until Miss Blodgett has had a chance to get on some clothes and pull herself together a little?'' Chambrun asked.

Hardy, a handkerchief wrapped around his hand, picked up the telephone on the bedside table. ''I'll join you as soon as my people get here,'' he said.

I gathered up Martha's meager belongings and we headed for the elevators. She walked, barefoot, between Chambrun and me, hanging on to each of us for support.

When we got to Chambrun's office, Betsy Ruysdale was there. I'll never know how Ruysdale manages it. No matter what the time of day or night, if there is a situation where Chambrun needs her, she manages to be on tap.

There is a little dressing room and bath off Chambrun's office. He uses it for normal needs and for an occasional forty winks in the course of a busy day. He actually lives in a penthouse on the roof. Ruysdale took Martha's things from me, and without any questions led her away.

In the office Chambrun went to his desk and the phone. He called the security office and talked to Bill Plante, Jerry Dodd's chief of staff. ''I want a report on Terrence Cleaves,'' he said, ''from the moment he left Mark's apartment at a little after two o'clock this morning.'' Plante's report was brief, and Chambrun thanked him and put down the phone. ''Cleaves went directly to his room, 805, and hasn't left it since.''

''You thought—?''

"He had a motive," Chambrun said. "Andrews was out to get him. Did Mrs. Cleaves tell you anything?"

I tried to make Connie's story sound sensible. About all it did was verify the fact that Terrence Cleaves had something serious to hide, just as Colin Andrews had told us.

"Something about it doesn't add up," Chambrun said, scowling at the end of his cigarette. "She has something on Cleaves, something big. It would seem she could get custody of her children and walk out on him. But she stays with him, even though they 'loathe' each other, she told you."

"It's hard to figure," I said.

"I am also bothered by an echo," Chambrun said. "Andrews told you that Cleaves found his wife in bed with a young man in the foreign service, beat him half to death. Tonight someone finds Miss Blodgett in bed with Andrews and does beat him to death. Miss Blodgett indicated to you that Cleaves had been after her. What was it she said about her track shoes being worn out? You'd say Cleaves doesn't like other men to fool around with women he considers belong to him. But unless Bill Plante slipped up, it could have been Cleaves who broke into 1014."

"He could have slipped up," I said.

"I almost wish I thought so," Chambrun said. "It would make it so simple."

Ruysdale emerged from the dressing room at that point. She is a woman who rarely shows any sort of deep feeling, but she looked a little done in this time.

"That's a very gutsy girl," she said to Chambrun. "Go easy with her, Pierre. She's hanging on by an eyelash."

I can't remember ever having heard her call him by his first name before.

"Will you call Bill Plante," Chambrun said. "He says Cleaves has been covered every minute of the time since he left Mark's apartment. I want the details of that coverage, minute by minute. If there is the tiniest gap in it, I want to know."

While he was talking, Jerry Dodd came into the office.

"You think Cleaves got away from us?" he asked.

Chambrun told him why he was wondering.

"I followed him from Mark's apartment," Jerry said. "Your orders. I saw him go into 805. I called Bill Plante on the hall phone. The door to 805 was never out of my sight. Bill sent up two men—that's how important I thought it was after looking at Mrs. Cleaves! Not for any reason were those two guys to leave their post together. If they did, God help them."

"Anything new in 1014?" Chambrun asked.

Jerry's mouth twisted down at the corners. "Some kind of a maniac," he said. "That poor bastard was slugged fifteen or twenty times—long after he was dead of it. It's a wonder the girl was left alive, in case she saw him."

"He obviously wasn't interested in the girl, except to keep her from identifying him. Weapon?"

"Nothing in the room. The killer took it away with him. And he must have walked down the tenth-floor corridor spattered with blood. No way he could have avoided getting it all over him."

"And nobody saw him," Chambrun said.

"Four-thirty—quarter to five in the morning. Not many people up and around. We're not covering the fire stairs except from Fourteen to Sixteen."

"Have you checked whether anybody has come or gone from Coriander's party?"

"We were told to let people come and go at will," Jerry said. "But my men have orders to report to me any movement up or down from Fifteen, with descriptions of who. The only people since early morning to move in and out of Fifteen are the room service waiters and Mark. They seem to be sitting very tight up there."

"So we take all your reports at face value, Jerry, and the killer in 1014 wasn't Cleaves and wasn't anyone from Coriander's army of occupation."

"Could be someone working for him on the outside."

"Why?" Chambrun asked.

"You got me."

"It could have no connection with our big troubles," Chambrun said. He glanced toward the door of the dressing room. "See if Miss Blodgett can join us, Mark."

I went over and knocked on the door. "Can we talk to you now, Martha?" I called out.

"In a minute."

I went across the office to Ruysdale's quarters. She was just putting down her phone.

"I'd appreciate it if you could look in on Mrs. Cleaves," I said. "She doesn't know why I've left her alone."

"Any connection between her beating and this new horror?" Ruysdale asked.

"Not one we've been able to make," I said. "If you could find a pair of dark glasses for her; she'll want to hide her eyes."

"You're a nice boy, Mark," Ruysdale said.

Nobody had called me a boy for a very long time.

I got back into Chambrun's office just as Martha Blodgett came out of the dressing room. "Gutsy," Ruysdale had called her. She looked fresh and in control. A Band-Aid was visible under her hairline, but otherwise she was perfectly put together.

"Some coffee or a drink?" Chambrun asked her.

"Some coffee with just a little bourbon in it," Martha said.

Jerry Dodd went to the sideboard to get it for her. There's always coffee there, Turkish for Chambrun and in an American percolator for the more civilized. Martha sat down in a Windsor chair near Chambrun's desk.

"There's one thing I want to say to you, Mr. Chambrun, before you ask me questions," she said.

"You have the floor," Chambrun said. His bright eyes were squinted against the smoke from his cigarette.

"I'm not ashamed of what I did tonight," Martha said. "I'm not ashamed that I went to bed with Colin and that we made love together for a long, lovely time."

"Why should you be?" Chambrun asked.

"We belong to different generations, Mr. Chambrun. Your generation has different sexual morals from mine. There's nothing in my code that makes going to bed with a man on your first date with him a sin."

A small smile moved Chambrun's lips. "I think the only difference between your time and mine, Miss Blodgett, is that we talked a very good game of strict behavior, but we paid no attention to what we pretended to believe. I suspect that first dates wound up

in lovemaking just as often as they do now. You are
open and frank about it, which I think is a little
healthier than we were. Perhaps, sometime, we can
discuss the matter a little more fully and under pleas-
anter circumstances. But right now we need help from
you. You say this was your first date with Andrews?"

She held her head very high. "The first date that
could have ended in bed," she said. "I knew him. He
bought me lunch a couple of times. He was working
on a story about Terrence Cleaves, my boss. At first I
resented his thinking that I might leak some information to him. I had no use for Cleaves as a human
being. I told you he kept me busy ducking—and every
other girl on the staff. But he was brilliant at his job
and I owed him loyalty. But Colin told me things that
made me wonder about Cleaves. Colin asked me to
watch for any contacts or special meetings he might
have with Far Eastern people—Chinese, Cambodi-
ans, Laotians, Thais. Colin was certain he had sold
out to someone who might have Communist lean-
ings. And so I watched for him—and we lunched again
a few times. Then tonight—" She stopped to sip her
coffee and brandy.

"Someone later is going to ask you the right questions about Cleaves, what you found out and passed
on to Andrews. But right now I'm concerned only
about tonight."

She nodded. "As you know, Mr. Chambrun, we
were locked out of our rooms on the fifteenth floor.
The management found us other rooms. Mine was
1014. We weren't all together any more, the staff. We
were scattered around. The story was out, the kidnapping, the demands. Cleaves had naturally left the
United Nations and come flying back here. I came

with him in case he had orders for me. It turned out
there was nothing I could do. I just waited around, in
the restaurants and the bars, trying to gather what
news I could. Everybody had a story, a new piece of
gossip about what was being done or not done to res-
cue the children and Katherine Horn. In the middle of
the evening I ran into Colin in the Trapeze Bar. We sat
and talked, as well as we could in all the noise, and he
told me his theory: that Cleaves had kidnapped his
own children in order to raise a fortune for himself.''

"Did you buy it?" Chambrun asked.

"Let me say I thought Cleaves was capable of it—at
least of thinking of it. I knew he couldn't be the Coriander Mark was said to have seen. I was with Cleaves
when that was going on. I couldn't believe he was head
of this fantastic Army For Justice. I think I thought he
might play along with them for a solid share of the
profits.''

"Did you tell Andrews that?"

"I didn't really have a chance. Maybe I hadn't
thought it through then. Anyway, Mark joined us then
and he invited us to his apartment for a drink, where
we could talk and hear ourselves think. Mark was
concerned about Connie Cleaves, who was missing.
We never got back to talking about Colin's theory.
You called to say that Mr. Ames was on his way, and
we left Mark." She stopped, her lips quivering slightly.
Chambrun waited for her to go on. "Colin had tried
to get a room in the hotel so he could be near the center of action. There were no rooms. And so—and
so—"

"You invited him to share yours."

"I knew what would happen if he said yes," Martha said, her voice growing unsteady. "I wanted it to

happen. He smiled at me and said he'd be glad to accept my hospitality. There—there wasn't anything to talk about. He didn't have to romance me. We went up to my room—and I went into the bathroom. I—I undressed and put on the robe I'd bought at the boutique earlier in the day. When I came back into the room, Colin was in my bed and we—we came together. It—it was marvelous, the best I've ever had in a sort of hit-and-miss sex life. We slept a little, and then we made love again, and then Colin screamed and rolled away from me. All—all I saw was a dark shadow and then something smashed down on my head and I blacked out.'' She drew a long breath. ''When I—revived—I found Colin—the way you saw him—and called Mark.''

After a moment Chambrun asked: ''Did you talk any further about Andrews' Cleaves theory?''

''My dear Mr. Chambrun, we talked about nothing except how marvelous it was to be a man and a woman—together.''

''You never had any sexual dealings with Cleaves?'' Chambrun asked.

''My God, no.''

''Is there some other man who might care so much for you he would kill any man he found in your bed?''

''In a way I wish I could say 'yes' to that. I mean—well, I've never been that important to anyone—unfortunately.''

''When you were assigned to 1014 you were given a key at the desk, or by the bellboy who took you upstairs. Did you lose that key? Or leave it inside your room and have to ask the desk for another?''

''No. The key was in my purse. The detective found it there, remember?''

"I wanted to make sure that wasn't a second key," Chambrun said. "You see, the killer found a key to let himself in. If he didn't steal it from you, then he had to get it from the desk."

"Have you thought that Terrence Cleaves must have been desperately afraid that Colin would come up with something provable about him?" Martha asked.

"I have. But I also have to tell you that Cleaves was being watched and that he couldn't have been the man who broke into your room."

She sat very still, a frown creasing her forehead. I thought she looked like a very puzzled small child. "There is a young, quite attractive Chinese man, head of some sort of trade commission, who lives here in the hotel, Mr. Chambrun. I think his name is Lu-Feng. We call him Mr. Lu. I told you Colin had asked me to keep an eye on any Far Eastern contacts Cleaves had. He saw Mr. Lu quite often, had cocktails with him here in the Lounge and in the Trapeze Bar. You know him?"

"Lu-Feng has been staying here for about a month," Chambrun said. He pressed the intercom button on his desk. "Ruysdale, get me the registration file on Lu-Feng, please." He leaned back in his chair. "What interests you about Mr. Lu, Martha?"

"Well—only that if Colin was right, and Cleaves sold out to someone, then the person he sold out to would be in trouble, too, wouldn't he? He'd want Colin out of the way just as badly as Cleaves might, wouldn't he?"

"Possibly. Did you find anything in investigating for Andrews that made you think Mr. Lu might be the man Andrews was after?"

"No. Just that he is a Chinese, a Communist, and that Cleaves saw a good deal of him. Mr. Chambrun?"

"Yes?"

"Do you think what happened to Colin has anything to do with Coriander and the children and all that?"

"I wish to God I knew," Chambrun said.

PART THREE

ONE

IT WAS ABOUT seven in the morning and I had left
Chambrun's office and gone back to my own apartment. I needed to shave and shower and get myself
some clean clothes.

Ruysdale was there when I let myself in, and she indicated, fingers to her lips, that Connie was asleep. I
tiptoed into the bathroom and got my shaving gear.
Clean clothes would have to wait. I went back to
Chambrun's office and asked to use his dressing room.
Chambrun was attacking an almost raw breakfast
steak with hot rolls, sweet butter, and honey on the
side. It was a standard breakfast for him, although a
little earlier than usual. He usually had this hearty
breakfast about eight and didn't eat again till dinner-
time.

He handed me a registration card as I stopped at his
desk. It was a dossier on Mr. Lu-Feng. The Chinese
businessman, head of a trade commission, was just
thirty years old, a graduate of Southern California in
business administration, unmarried, credit unlimited,
no bad marks. He had played on the golf team at
Southern Cal, and he had spent two years in London
for his trade commission before he'd come to New
York about a month ago.

"About all it does for us," Chambrun said, "is to
tell us that he was in London about the time Terrence
Cleaves was scratching for money to save himself. If
there's anything to Andrews' theory that Cleaves sold

out, Mr. Lu could have been a buyer. No proof whatsoever, of course."

"How can you approach him?" I asked.

"I can't. But at a decent hour you might have a try at it. He may have known Andrews in London. It would be logical to ask him anything he might know about Andrews and his connections, and in the process you could get around to Cleaves. Don't press too hard, but let me know your reactions."

"What do you think the next move will be from Coriander?" I asked him.

"If he's listening to radio or television, he knows that the President will make some sort of announcement about nine o'clock. He may buy what the President has to say. Personally, I doubt it. He'll know it's a stall and he'll probably insist on some kind of quick action from us."

"What kind of action?"

"Something he can believe," Chambrun said.

I went into the dressing room. No clean clothes, but I decided a shower after shaving would make me feel more human. The dressing room is soundproofed so that I had no way of knowing that anything was going on in Chambrun's office until I had dressed again and walked out there.

Chambrun was in the midst of being subjected to some high-pitched shouting by Buck Ames.

"I'll kill the sonofabitch!" the Buccaneer was announcing at the top of his lungs. "Lay his hands on Connie, will he? I'll give it back to him in spades! Double spades!" He started for the door.

"Wait!" Chambrun said sharply. When he gave an order, even Buck Ames hesitated. "You've only heard part of the evening's story, Buck.'' And Chambrun told him about Colin Andrews' bloody passing.

Some kind of juices seemed to run out of the older man. He grabbed the back of a chair for support. The fury that had driven him a moment before seemed to have evaporated.

"He was a real square shooter, Andrews," Buck said. "Any leads?"

"Before you start thinking of an obvious one," Chambrun said, "let me tell you that the one thing we know for certain is that it wasn't Cleaves. He was being watched at the time."

"I—I'd better go to Connie," Buck said. I had a feeling he was thinking less about her than something else that had come as a shock to him.

"She's asleep," I said. "She needs whatever rest she can get."

"My secretary's with her," Chambrun said. "Far more important, Buck, is that we're going to need answers for Coriander within a couple of hours. What luck have you had with the money side of this thing?"

Buck actually moved around the chair he'd been hanging onto and sat down. "It's a squeeze," he said.

"What kind of a squeeze?"

"My people will get up the money if—and it's an almost impossible if."

" 'Impossible' is a big word under the conditions," Chambrun said.

"It's a long list," Buck said. "Certain oil leases, access to raw materials, guarantees that certain contracts will come their way."

"Who has to say yes to those demands?"

"The government," Buck said. "They're no more likely to go for that than they are for Coriander's political demands. The goddamned money is right there, could be had today. But we're not going to get it.'' He drew a deep breath and squared his shoulders. ''I told you there's just one way to fight an army, Chambrun, and that's with an army. I can supply the troops.''

''What kind of contact does Cleaves have with your people?'' Chambrun said.

''They wouldn't give him a peanut-stand concession,'' Buck said. ''He's been to the well once, when he had his big trouble, and they laughed at him.''

''If Cleaves and Coriander are in this together—'' Chambrun said thoughtfully. ''Is it possible they made an advance deal with ITC knowing that you'd go to ITC for the money? I gather two hundred and fifty million would not be an inflated price for ITC to pay for what it wants.''

''Jesus!'' Buck said. He didn't say ''yes'' or ''no'' or ''maybe.''

Chambrun ground out his cigarette in the ash tray on his desk. I could always tell when he was going to start on a new line.

''What has Cleaves got on you, Buck?'' he asked.

The Buccaneer's head jerked up. ''What the hell are you talking about?'' he said.

''Your daughter has been a puzzle to me from the start, Buck,'' Chambrun said. ''Her marriage is no good. She has been publicly humiliated by Cleaves. But she stays with him.''

''The children,'' Buck said. ''And being a damn fool woman she probably still has a yen for him.''

''Not good enough,'' Chambrun said. ''Cleaves's position in politics makes a scandal something he would avoid. A noisy divorce would do him real damage. For the early part of the marriage he seems to have behaved himself. Suddenly he starts running wild, chasing every skirt in sight, bringing women home to his house and flaunting them in front of his wife, humiliating and degrading her.

"Because she was having herself a fling," Buck said.

"I don't think so," Chambrun said. "She was driven into someone's bed, finally, but I think that was after Cleaves had blown his stack. I have tried to imagine what possible reason she could have for staying with Cleaves and I've come to a conclusion about it. You are the closest and dearest person to Constance in the whole world. I think Cleaves has something on you, Buck, and she knows it. She's stayed with him, put up with it all, because she knows if she doesn't, Cleaves has it in his power to ruin you. He holds it over her head, and she'll protect you no matter what the pain. He beats her cruelly and she won't bring charges against him—because of you, Buck."

The Buccaneer stood up, and his lithe body shook like a man with the ague. "That is pure bullshit, Chambrun!" he said. He turned to me. "Please take me to Connie, Haskell. I don't intend to listen to any more of this kind of crap."

I glanced at Chambrun and his shoulders rose in a slight shrug. Wondering, I took Buck Ames down the hall to my apartment.

CONNIE WAS UP and dressed and sipping some coffee Ruysdale had made for her in the kitchenette. She was wearing a large pair of dark glasses that hid her eyes. Good old Ruysdale.

When she saw Buck, Connie sprang up out of her chair and ran into his arms. He held her, gently, while she cried a little, her face buried against his shoulder. He kept saying "Baby, Baby," over and over. There could be no doubt these two people loved each other very much.

Ruysdale discreetly headed for the door and I started to follow her.

"Wait, please, Haskell," Buck said.

He took Connie toward the couch and they sat down together, his arm around her. I waited, standing across the room by the door. I might as well have been a piece of furniture for all the attention they paid to me.

"Cleaves did this to you, Baby?" Buck asked.

"It doesn't matter, Buck," she said.

"I am going to kill him," Buck said as matter-of-factly as though he were saying he was going to the supermarket for a pound of butter. Maybe she was used to his extravaganzas, because she didn't react.

"Mark told me you were trying to find the money," she said. "Is it possible, Buck?"

"Possible," he said, not telling her the whole truth.

"Thank God," she said. The dark glasses turned my way. "Is there any news from—from upstairs, Mark?"

"Nothing," I said. "The President is going to make a statement of some sort at nine o'clock. After that perhaps."

Buck spoke very casually. "Chambrun thinks you are staying with that louse because he has something on me and is forcing you to stay to protect me. Anything to it?"

She turned her head sharply to look at him. "Of course not," she said in a very small voice.

I knew, right then, that she was lying. Was it possible that she had kept whatever it was from Buck?

That he really didn't know? It was that, or he was a superb actor.

"You tell your boss he's full of it," Buck said to me.

"Mark has been so very kind to me," Connie said. "Would you like me to clear out, Mark?"

"Just give me five minutes in the bedroom for a clean shirt and a pressed suit," I said.

While I was changing in the bedroom, I thought we were dealing with a very neat double blackmail. Cleaves had something on Buck and was using it to maneuver Connie. And Connie had something on her husband and was prepared to use it if it came to a showdown—something so important Cleaves had turned violent to stop her.

It was all part of this time of terror that threatened the lives of two children, Katherine Horn, and the hotel itself. Horween and Andrews had died violently as the wheels turned. The big payoff was still ahead of us and it appeared we had no way of meeting it on any sort of equal ground.

I CHECKED WITH Room Service and learned that Mr. Lu-Feng, in room 1122, had ordered breakfast about ten minutes ago. The room service waiter was just backing out of Mr. Lu's room when I arrived there.

Martha Blodgett had called Mr. Lu "attractive," and he was. He was medium height, lean and hard physically. He received me with what seemed to be a perpetual smile. There was nothing of the Oriental mystique about him. His speech was entirely American and quite colloquial.

He invited me to join him for coffee while he had his very American breakfast of ham and eggs and hard rolls. He had ordered a double coffee for himself and Room Service had sent him two cups.

"I'm not usually up at this time of day," he told me. "But the excitement you've provided here in the hotel has us all a little jumpy, I guess. What can I do for you, Mr. Haskell?"

"Information about a man named Colin Andrews," I said.

"*London Times*," he said. "One of the better political journalists. I saw him quite often when I was stationed in London."

"He was murdered here in the hotel in the early hours of this morning," I said.

The smile remained frozen on Mr. Lu's mouth, but it had left his slanted brown eyes. "You're kidding," he said. "Who? How?"

"He was beaten to death," I said. "'Who' is what we need help with. Mr. Chambrun guessed that you had known Andrews in London and hoped you might be able to tell us something about his friends. Perhaps I should say his enemies."

Mr. Lu seemed to have lost interest in what remained of his ham and eggs. He lifted a napkin to his mouth and held it there for a moment. "I don't like to dish out any dirt about someone who's already got enough trouble," he said. "And it is just dirt—nothing factual."

I waited for him to go on.

"I happen to know," he said, "Andrews was working on a story about Terrence Cleaves. What I think newspapermen call an 'in depth' story. If he had turned up anything damaging to Cleaves—"

"Maybe I can make it easier for you," I said. "The one thing we do know about Andrews' murder is that

Terrence Cleaves didn't kill him. He was being watched by our security people at the important time."

"Why?" Mr. Lu asked, his eyes very bright.

That, I decided, was not for publication. "All the key people concerned with the kidnapping are being kept under surveillance."

"So that's that," Mr. Lu said.

"How did you know about the story Andrews was preparing to write?" I asked him.

"He interviewed me. Once in London, once here in New York about a week ago."

"What did he hope you could tell him?"

Mr. Lu's smile was back in working order. "I've known Terry Cleaves quite well for the last several years," he said. "Before he was appointed Ambassador to the U.N. he was a special consultant to the Prime Minister on Far Eastern affairs. I was concerned with certain trade negotiations with the British government. Terry was the man I dealt with at that time, he and his chief aide, a guy named Horween. Horween is a former secret agent for the British and he knows my part of the world like the back of his hand."

I managed to keep my mouth shut about Horween.

"Big business is rarely conducted in offices," Mr. Lu said. "Terry and I lunched and dined together often. We played golf together." The smile widened. "I lost more golf matches to him that I could easily have won than I can count. Beating me made him feel kindly."

"So Andrews knew you were Cleaves's friend?"

"It was no secret. Andrews was interested in Cleaves's finances. You know that he was in trouble for a while?"

"The T.C. 4," I said.

Mr. Lu laughed. "I bought one of those cars to keep Terry feeling cordial. I was one of a very few, I'm afraid. It's a marvelous car, by the way, but too expensive for a mass success. Andrews thought I might be able to tell him how Terry got out of his jam."

"Could you?"

Mr. Lu shrugged. "I gave Andrews my best guess," he said. "Walter Ames—Buck Ames. Ames isn't a very rich man, but he works for some of the richest and most powerful men in the world."

"International Trade Corporation."

"A powerhouse in the world of finance. My guess was that Buck Ames got up the dough for Terry in return for some undercover political favors for ITC."

"You think ITC bailed Cleaves out," I said.

"My very best guess," Mr. Lu said.

"You didn't know that Buck Ames hates Cleaves's guts?" I asked.

"Business and personal likes and dislikes don't have much to do with each other," Mr. Lu said. "Business is business. If Buck Ames could make a good deal for his people, he wouldn't let his feelings for his son-in-law stand in the way. Besides, he would have been helping to keep his daughter from going down with the ship."

"You know her—Mrs. Cleaves?"

"I met her just once," Mr. Lu said. "At a formal embassy party. A beautiful woman. Not one I would like to lose if she were mine."

"There was gossip about her, I'm told."

Mr. Lu gave me a wise look. "If I wanted to know about that, I'd ask the manager of the Beaumont to let me look at the records he keeps on his guests. I understand some of the shrewdest dossiers on important people are right in Mr. Chambrun's files."

I dodged that needle. "I asked you about gossip, not what the truth is," I said.

"Oh, there was gossip," Mr. Lu said. "She was seen around London, at the most posh clubs and hotel restaurants with a variety of escorts. People like to think that a glamor girl like Constance Cleaves is up to no good." He chuckled. "People assumed that Cleaves's job at Downing Street made it impossible to do much socializing. Beautiful wife left to her own devices choosing to live it up a little isn't unheard of."

"But Cleaves's job wasn't keeping him occupied?"

Mr. Lu sipped his coffee and made an unhappy face. It was cold. "I thought you came here to ask about Colin Andrews," he said. "Poor bastard. Where did it happen?"

I cleaned it up for him. "He was having a nightcap with a girl named Martha Blodgett in her room. Someone broke in. She was slugged before she got a look at the killer. When she came to, she found Andrews dead."

The slant eyes narrowed. "The Blodgett girl works on Terry's staff, doesn't she? Andrews was still digging for his story?"

"That seems to have been it," I said.

"I can only tell you this, Haskell. Terry was involved in a lot of top hush-hush diplomatic maneuverings. If Andrews was getting close to something that would embarrass the British government, the big boys wouldn't hesitate to get rid of him. Beating him to death in front of a possible witness is a little crude, but governments, out of the public view, don't hesitate to silence people who may be dangerous to them.

The British government, your government, mine; secret agents, CIA people, our terror groups. I'd have to guess Andrews was about to strike oil and someone had to stop him." He looked at me steadily for a moment. "Your Mr. Chambrun must be wondering if Andrews' murder has anything to do with what's going on with this Army For Justice."

"Your guess?"

He grinned at me. "In my opinion everything in the world is related to everything else in the world. This is closer than any such broad generalization. Andrews was hunting down Cleaves's history; Cleaves's children are kidnapped. That's a connection. Where it leads, who knows?" He glanced at his watch. "But the wheels are about to start turning, Haskell. Your President will speak in about an hour. After that your Mr. Coriander will laugh himself sick at the obvious attempt to deceive him. Then he will act, unpleasantly for the children, I'm afraid, unless you have some way to stop him."

"How would you handle it if you had the decision to make?" I asked him.

The smile was entirely gone for the first time now. He took a cigarette out of his pocket and lit it with a jade lighter. "I would recruit the strongest force of specialists I could," he said. "Experts with handguns, machine pistols, explosives—even electronics to deal with that detonator that was described in the press. I would go in on a prearranged signal and hope that the few seconds of time surprise might give me would make it possible to disconnect the detonator."

"And save the children and Miss Horn," I said. "You'd be gambling on a few seconds, as you say."

He shook his head. "If I had the decision to make, Haskell, I would have some kind of sympathetic person on hand to console the children's grief-stricken mother. I'm afraid I don't think you'll ever get them out in one piece—I mean, alive."

TWO

IT WAS A QUARTER to nine.

A strange group of people were waiting in Chambrun's office for the words of the President of the United States. Law and Order was represented by Gus Brand of the FBI, Assistant Commissioner Treadway, Captain Valentine of the bomb squad, Lieutenant Hardy of Homicide, and our own Jerry Dodd. There was Jim Priest of the State Department. The victims—the Cleaveses and Buck Ames—waited on opposite sides of the room, Buck with his arm around Connie, whose eyes were hidden by those black glasses, Cleaves playing that detached and expressionless Coldstream Guardsman. Miss Ruysdale stood behind Chambrun's desk, ready for any orders that might come. Chambrun was in his desk chair, apparently shut away inside himself. I knew him well enough to be certain that failure was eating away at his gut. All the people around him, with all their skills, with courage to spare, were helpless. Not one of them had the authority to meet any one of Coriander's demands. Buck Ames, looking drawn and pale, might find the money, but with unacceptable conditions attached.

At a couple of minutes to nine, Miss Ruysdale turned on the portable TV set that had been brought into the office and placed it against the far wall. Commercials for some underarm spray were on. And then, from the Oval Office of the White House, the chief executive's press secretary introduced the President.

His speech was short, delivered in a low, concerned voice. His listeners, he was certain, were all aware of the kidnapping of the Cleaves children and Miss Horn, and of the ransom demands being made by a man who called himself Colonel Coriander and the Army For Justice. The President said he felt certain the money demands could be met. But, he said, the other demands were far more difficult to meet in any reasonably short period of time. They involved diplomatic negotiations that must take place halfway round the world. He urged Coriander to give him the necessary time to carry out those negotiations. He urged the "thousands of demonstrators" who were expressing their sympathy with Coriander's political demands to recognize their complexity and to be patient while he gave the problem his "best efforts." He suggested prayers for the children and for their parents and relatives, "sick with anxiety." Time and patience were the key to the problem, he told his audience.

That was it.

There was an instant babble of conversation in the room, interrupted by the blinking red eye on Chambrun's telephone. Miss Ruysdale switched off the TV set on which some news analyst was paraphrasing the President's speech.

"Quiet!" Jerry Dodd called out.

Chambrun leaned forward and switched on the squawk box on his desk. "Chambrun here," he said.

Coriander's mocking voice came through the box. "Having listened to that remarkable double-talk from the Great White Father," he said, "it is time for action. Send Haskell up here and I'll tell him exactly what must be done and how. Ten minutes from now."

Connie Cleaves broke away from her father and ran toward the desk. "He's got to let me go up with Mark!" she said. "I'm happy to be an extra hostage, but please, for God's sake, let me be with the children."

"You heard, Coriander?" Chambrun asked.

"I heard, but the answer is no," Coriander said. "I don't choose to have a pleading and weeping woman hanging around my neck. Haskell and nobody else."

The phone clicked off.

"He saw through it," Gus Brand said. "That leaves us only one choice."

"What choice?" Connie asked.

"We go in praying," Brand said.

"You've got to wait to hear what he tells Mark!" she said. "You've got to!"

"It will take us a while to get organized, Mrs. Cleaves."

"You've got to give my children a chance," she said, desperate. "If you try to force your way in, he will kill everyone before you can reach them."

"Would you prefer to have them killed inch by inch, piece by piece?" Brand asked in a cold voice. "There's not very much chance our way, Mrs. Cleaves, but it's better than having your children tortured while we do nothing."

"He's right, Baby," Buck Ames said. He had reached Connie and had his protecting arm around her again.

Gus Brand was confronting me. "You will of course listen carefully to what he has to tell you, Haskell. But almost more important is for you to be able to tell us

every detail of what you see. Are the girls and Miss
Horn being kept in the same room where you saw
them before? Most essential for us to know, is the
detonator still in the same room where you saw it yesterday morning? Count heads. How many people do
you see this time? Are the hallways guarded now?
Approach it as though it was your first time up there.
Understand? Because when we move, we'll want to hit
the detonator and the children without making any
false moves.''

"I understand," I said. "But I'll see just what Coriander wants me to see—no more, no less.''

"Get clever," Brand said.

Chambrun looked up at me from his desk. "Pay
careful attention to Coriander," he said.

"I will.''

"I don't mean to what he says, Mark. I want you to
use your eyes. Is he the same man you talked to the
first time? Is that sleeve empty because he has no arm,
or is it part of the disguise and does he have an arm
held against his body inside the robe? We're checking
army records for an amputee. He may not be an amputee at all.''

"Interesting point," Brand said, "but it isn't going
to make much difference who he is when we go in.''

"Just in case he comes out and you don't," Chambrun said. He sounded suddenly very tired. "There are
two things I don't believe, Mr. Brand. I don't believe
you can surprise him, and I don't believe he hasn't
planned an escape route for himself.''

"You think—?''

"I think he may kill the children and blow up the
hotel," Chambrun said, "but I don't think he'll be in
the wreckage.''

"We've got every possible way out covered, boss," Jerry Dodd said.

"All he has to do is get to another floor," Chambrun said. "Without the kid's mask, the fright wig, and the empty sleeve he can walk right past us like any other hotel guest."

"The fire stairs from Fifteen, up and down, are guarded," Jerry said.

"So we may wind up with some dead security men," Chambrun said. "I wouldn't bet a plugged nickel against his chances of getting away if he wants to."

"No one is going to get past us without proper identification," Brand said.

"You're going to check on a thousand guests coming and going?" Chambrun sounded bitter. "You don't have the manpower. It will turn out he's already registered as a guest in the hotel and he will have the proper credentials to prove he's one of a thousand innocent bystanders."

"He said ten minutes, Mark," Connie said. "Please, please try to see Liz and Mariella."

"I'll do my best," I said.

"What you see and hear may be the difference between success and failure, Haskell," Brand said. "Good luck."

"I'll see you around—I hope," I said.

The lobby was buzzing with excitement again. I suppose everyone in the hotel had heard the President's speech. I was instantly surrounded by the ladies and gentlemen of the press. We were supposed to have had a press conference at nine o'clock. The President's speech had put that off, and as a matter of fact I'd forgotten all about it. Now they were thirsty for information. I told them I was on my way up to talk to Coriander. After that there might be news.

I had to fight my way through them to get to the west wing elevators. The operator took me to Fifteen. This was my third trip up there and the sensation of panic I felt was no less from having done it before. The corridors were still deserted. The linen room door on the west side swayed slightly in a gentle breeze from an open window.

I walked around to the north side, to the door of 15 A. I knocked. The delay was longer than it had been the other times. Finally the door was opened and I was confronted by the bizarre image of Coriander in his false face, the wild wig, and the empty sleeve. I found myself staring at that sleeve, telling myself if he really had an arm he couldn't help moving it inside the robe—unless it was strapped to his side. The robe was a loose-hanging thing. I couldn't tell anything for sure.

"You took your time," Coriander said.

"I had to fight my way through an army of news-paper people," I said.

"And of course there were your instructions from Chambrun and Gus Brand and the tears and pleas of Connie-baby."

The sonofabitch knew everything. He gestured me into the living room.

"I've been very patient, Haskell," he said. There were no overtones of mockery in his voice now.

"You're asking for a lot. It takes time trying to meet your demands."

"That's a lot of balls and you know it," he said. He sat down on the end of the stretcher table, one leg swinging free. "The only person who has made any kind of an effort is Buck Ames, and he's come up with impossible demands. As impossible as mine.''

''So you know you're asking for something we can't deliver,'' I said.

''Oh, you could deliver if there was a spark of honesty in any of you,'' he said. ''You have allowed thousands of decent, honest men to be thrown into torture dungeons in Indochina. If you had a spark of honesty you would admit you were wrong and set them free. You brought our prisoners of war home, and to hell with anyone else. That is called honor!'' His laugh was bitter. ''The men who ordered the cold-blooded murder of civilians in Vietnam are sitting in their plush offices laughing at me and my demands. Buck Ames can find the money I ask for if he will sell out his country to the private bandits. But you could find clean money for me if there was a drop of compassion in any of you. Because I will destroy those children, Haskell.''

''I want to see them,'' I said.

''You'll see them,'' he said. ''But it will be the last time anyone will see them alive and whole unless I'm given what I ask for by the end of the business day today.''

''You know that's simply not possible,'' I said.

''Oh, I'm reducing my demands,'' he said, cheerfully swinging his leg. ''I give you till the end of the business day today to raise the money. If you have raised it and it's in my hands, you will give us free passage out of the hotel, a plane to fly us to Cuba. We will, of course, have the two little girls and Miss Horn with us. One false move and we will splatter their little brains on the sidewalk.''

''When do you turn them loose?'' I asked.

"When at least some portion of my other demands are met—a portion satisfactory to me."

"I can try," I said.

He leaned forward and I could see the glitter of eyes behind the holes in the false face. "I want you to understand just what cards I hold, Haskell. I know, for instance, that you were ordered to look me over very carefully to make certain that I really don't have a left arm. I know that you were ordered to make sure of where the girls are kept, and whether the detonator you saw on your first visit is still in 1507. I know that Gus Brand and his FBI boys are planning a break-in and they want to be certain where those key locations are. I know that your very wise Mr. Chambrun thinks I have arranged a way out of here for myself. Since I know all those things, Haskell, do you imagine I won't know of any double-cross you're planning for me? Are those cards enough to make for a winning hand, would you say?"

I think my jaw must have sagged open. He might just as well have been in Chambrun's office twenty minutes ago. The only explanation I could think of was that Chambrun's office was bugged. Why would he tell me all this if that was so? He must know that the minute I got back downstairs—if I got back downstairs—the bug would be discovered and put out of commission.

"The money thing is quite simple," Coriander said. His voice was amused again. It must have been the expression on my face. "They will get it—all of it—in hundred-dollar bills. That's a fashionable denomination these days. It will be packed in no more suitcases than you can carry up here by yourself. With the money you will bring arrangements I can believe for our safe way out of the hotel with the hostages.''

"And if you're not satisfied?" It was a mouse squeak from me.

"If I'm not satisfied, friend, I will avail myself of the escape route Mr. Chambrun imagines I have, but not before I blow up this floor of the hotel with the hostages and you on board, Haskell. I urge you not to involve yourself in tricks. I have nothing against you. But the bearer of false promises will be dealt with like the old-time Greek bearer of bad news. Now, come have a last look at the girls. You haven't much time to waste. The end of the business day for the money, remember."

I was taken down the corridor to the bedroom where I'd first seen them. Elizabeth and Mariella were there alone, huddled together on a small love seat. Twenty-four hours had sapped them of most of their courage, I thought. The look of hope and expectation they gave me made me feel a little sick.

Katherine Horn wasn't with them.

"I'm happy to tell you," Coriander said at my elbow, "that the dark lady of the sonnets finally opted for pleasure."

I moved dry lips. "Your mother and father send their love," I said to the girls.

"You haven't come to get us?" Elizabeth asked.

"We still have to stay here?" Mariella asked.

"It takes time to make arrangements," I said. "You haven't been treated unkindly, have you?"

"We heard the President's speech," Elizabeth said.

"They don't think he was telling the truth," Mariella said. "I have told them if someone has to be hurt, it should be me. I can stand pain better than Liz."

God, they knew the whole thing, all the threats. I
saw the TV set in the corner of the room. They must
have been allowed to listen to it round the clock. The
news media hadn't left out a single gory possibility in
their coverage of the story. These kids knew exactly
what was in store for them if Coriander's demands
weren't met.

"I'll be back before the end of the day," I said.
"We'll have things worked out by then. No one will
have to be hurt." I tried to sound as though I believed
it.

"Tell Mum that we—" Elizabeth began.

"Tell her we know she's doing everything that can
be done," Mariella finished for her.

"Time's awasting," Coriander said.

I reached out and touched Mariella's hair, so like
her mother's. "Keep your cool," I said. "We're doing
everything we can. I'll be back, I promise."

I went back out into the living room with Coriander. I hadn't seen a sign of anyone else. The men in the
stocking masks were conspicuous by their absence.

"Don't come back without the money and the plan
for departure," Coriander said. "If you do, I'm afraid
you'll have to stay here for the payoff."

I was out in the hall by myself and running toward
the west wing. I went clattering down the fire stairs to
Fourteen, passing the two security men who were stationed there. They both knew me and they didn't stop
me for any chit-chat.

It took the elevator forever, it seemed, to come up
to Fourteen. The most urgent thing on my mind was
to get back to Chambrun's office and warn them that
the place was bugged. While they were making plans

for an attack on the fifteenth floor, Coriander was hearing every word they said.

I got awfully smart at that time, I thought. Instead of going direct to Chambrun's office, I went into my apartment down the hall. I called Chambrun on the house phone. He sounded impatient when he answered.

"Just listen to me without making any comments," I said. "Your office is bugged. Coriander hears everything that's going on in there. He knew you'd ordered me to try to make certain about his arm. He knew you'd told me to make certain where the girls were kept and if the detonator was still in 1507. He knew Brand is planning a break-in. He knew you were certain he'd planned an escape route for himself. He might just as well have been in the office with you."

"Come on back in," Chambrun said in a flat, emotionless voice.

Well, I'd warned him. Chambrun was right, of course. If I didn't return to the office and report, Coriander would know that I'd spilled the beans.

All the people who'd been in the office when I'd gone upstairs were still there. They were talking quite openly about the fact that the office might be bugged. Jerry Dodd was taking apart the telephone instruments on Chambrun's desk. Brand and Lieutenant Hardy were searching the baseboards, the light fixtures, the underside of Chambrun's desk, the pictures on the wall. I couldn't believe it.

Chambrun gave me a patient, paternal look. "He wouldn't have made it obvious to you, Mark, unless he expected you to tell us. He wanted you to tell us. There's no point in pretending you haven't."

Connie Cleaves wasn't concerned about electronics. She came directly to me; her hands groped for mine.

"You saw them?" she asked.

"They're all right," I said. "Unfortunately they know the whole story and they're quite naturally frightened."

"Coriander's threatened them?"

"There's a television set in the room and they've been listening. They know what Coriander has in mind for them."

"Oh, God!"

Gus Brand joined us. "They're in the same room?" he asked.

"Yes."

"Katherine Horn is still with them?"

"I didn't see her," I said. "Coriander suggested that she—she'd given in to certain sexual demands they'd made." I glanced at Cleaves. He was the completely expressionless Coldstream Guardsman. If he was shocked by the news, it didn't show on his rock-hard face. "There are new demands," I said.

The room went dead quiet as I told them. The money by the end of the business day, a way out for Coriander and his men and the children, probably Miss Horn, and a plane ready to fly them to Cuba. Coriander would wait for his other demands to be met when he was safely away from the hotel.

"A quarter of a billion dollars by five o'clock? He's off his rocker!" Buck Ames exploded.

Lieutenant Hardy wandered back into focus. "If there's a bug in this office, it's built into the cement walls," he said.

Chambrun nodded as though that was exactly what he'd expected. "I'm going to ask Mr. and Mrs. Cleaves and Mr. Ames to leave us while we decide what's to be done," he said.

"We have a right to know what you plan," Cleaves said in a dead voice.

"There is the money, Mr. Cleaves," Chambrun said. "You have less than seven hours in which to raise what you can. You, too, Buck. Don't shoot for the whole amount. Just get up what you can. Mr. Priest will work at it, too. When it's time to report to Coriander, we'll offer what we've got. Meanwhile we have to decide what the alternatives are if Coriander won't accept what we come up with. Ruysdale, you take Mrs. Cleaves back to Mark's apartment and stay with her."

Connie needed to hang onto Miss Ruysdale for support as they left the office. Cleaves and Buck Ames left without a word between them. They weren't going to be working together, that was for sure. When they were gone, Chambrun turned to me.

"How is the money to be delivered?" he asked.

"I take it," I said. "If we try to pull a fast one on him, I become a hostage, too."

Chambrun took a sip from the demitasse of Turkish coffee on his desk. "You don't have to do it," he said.

"You haven't seen those kids," I said. "But it's academic, isn't it? You can't raise the money."

Gus Brand took off his glasses and wiped them carefully. "Let's face the cold facts," he said. He held the glasses up to the light, was satisfied, and put them back on again. "We're not going to let him get away with it."

"Which is why I wanted the Cleaveses and Buck Ames out of here," Chambrun said. "Better they should be active than be tortured by that knowledge."

"I think you're all out of your minds," I said. "You haven't found a bug in here, but somehow he knows everything that's said in this office. You might as well tell him to go ahead and chop up the kids. You want pieces of them shipped down here to convince you he means business?"

"He's not hearing what goes on here," Chambrun said. He looked around at the tense faces—Priest, Treadway, Valentine, Hardy, Jerry Dodd. "Somebody reports it to him."

"How?" Priest asked. "Phone calls to the suite are monitored. There's been nothing. No one has come or gone except—" and he looked straight at me—"except Mark."

"And the room service waiters," Jerry said.

"Who have not heard anything that goes on in this room," Chambrun said.

"Then for God's sake how?" I said. "Because you know damn well I haven't told him anything."

"I'd like to think that," Priest said.

"Let's not waste time with nonsense," Chambrun said.

"Mark is struck with the lady," Priest said in a matter-of-fact voice. "He has a natural compassion for the children. He may have decided that cooperating with Coriander is the one way to save them. The last bit of cooperating will come when he goes up with whatever money we can raise and he tells Coriander what kind of trap we've set for him."

I felt cold sweat running down my back. "You're a crazy sonofabitch," I said.

"I'm pointing out the only possible explanation if there is no bug," Priest said.

"So there is a bug," I said. "You just haven't found it."

Priest smiled at me, a gentle smile. "In my business we learn to consider all possible alternatives, Mark," he said. "Suggest another one. No bug, not you, then how?"

"If we must theorize," Chambrun said, "then I offer one, Jim. Coriander has an ally on the outside. We know that ally doesn't communicate by phone; we know he hasn't been up to the fifteenth floor. So he has another way of communicating. I suggest some kind of walkie-talkie set."

"So one of us here in this room goes to the john and tells Coriander what's happening?" Brand asked.

"You suspect one of us?" Valentine asked, his jaw jutting toward Chambrun.

"It has to be someone who was in this room when we gave Mark instructions," Chambrun said.

Jerry Dodd laughed. "So we frisk each other for a walkie-talkie set—or look in the john for it."

"Not a bad idea to clear the air," Chambrun said, "but a waste of time. I don't suspect anyone here—now."

Brand gave him a steady look. "Cleaves? Ames?"

"Plus Mrs. Cleaves and Miss Ruysdale," Priest said. He sure did cover all the alternatives.

"It was suggested to us at the very beginning by the late Mr. Andrews that Cleaves might be Coriander, or working with Coriander," Chambrun said.

"That's really why you sent them away, isn't it, Pierre?" Priest said. "Not concern for their feelings."

"One of the reasons," Chambrun said. "There's no bug in this office. Coriander had to be in touch with someone who overheard the instructions we gave Mark. I happen to believe in all of you present, and in Miss Ruysdale."

"But nobody left this office while Mark was upstairs," Priest said.

"Several people went to the john while we waited to hear from Mark," Jerry Dodd said. "This situation kind of worked on bladders. God help me, I didn't keep track of who went and who didn't."

"Cleaves went," Hardy said. "I was fascinated with him. Not a word to his wife, not the smallest suggestion of sympathy for her."

"I think it's safe to say we can talk about what's to be done without its being relayed to Coriander," Chambrun said.

"What about Buck Ames? Could he be the one? His people work in devious ways," Priest said.

"At any rate he isn't here," Chambrun said. "So how do you see this situation, Mr. Brand?"

Brand moved around to stand by Chambrun's desk. On it were the blueprints of the building plus a floor plan. It was marked as the plan for the fifteenth floor, but all the floors above the second and up to the roof where there were penthouses were exactly the same.

"One of the most miserable parts of my job," Brand said, in his quiet, schoolteacher voice, "is to plan how to kill people. I think you all know that we aren't going to let Coriander get away with this. No way. We can't meet his demands, even if we were so inclined. The problem is, how to take him and still give the hostages some sort of outside chance of survival.''

"I find myself puzzled by one thing," Chambrun said. "Coriander must have known from the beginning that his political demands couldn't be met. The money demand is astronomical. He knew Cleaves couldn't meet it. Perhaps he thought public pressure from people who believed his political demands were genuine might help produce it. But he also had to know that the FBI would never let him walk away with whatever he got. He'd know you'd string it out as far as you could in the hope of saving the hostages. But you'd never let him go free. He starts out by trapping himself here in the hotel. With his bomb threat he probably thought the owners would help sweeten the pot to save their building from severe damage. In passing, I imagine they will. But he can't get out with anything—any political gains or any money. He'll be in range of your sharpshooters the minute he sticks his head out the door. If he adopts this second plan of taking the hostages to a waiting plane, he has to know he'll never get aboard it.''

"Thirty men could put up a pretty tough fight with the arms they've got—the arms Haskell saw," the Assistant Commissioner said.

"We don't know that there are thirty men," Chambrun said. "Mark has seen only two."

"We've fed thirty people," Jerry Dodd said.

"We've sent up thirty servings," Chambrun said. "That would include the hostages, which reduces the fighting men to twenty-seven. We have no way of being sure thirty servings were actually eaten. Food could be flushed down the drain. I have a strange feeling there is no army up there. Just three or four men.''

"The explosives are real and set in place," Valentine said. "Haskell saw them."

"That I believe," Chambrun said. "But it only takes one man—with one finger—to set them off."

"And kill himself when he does it," Valentine said.

"Not necessarily," Chambrun said. "There can be a time mechanism that Mark didn't spot. They leave the fifteenth floor by whatever the escape route is they have planned, and the bombs go off after they're out of danger. The danger to the hostages is just as real as we've always thought it was, but Coriander and his two or three soldiers walk right out past us."

"With empty pockets," Jim Priest said.

"Maybe not," Chambrun said. "He waits for Mark to bring him whatever money has been raised. It should be a substantial amount, enough for Coriander and his friends to live as rich men for the rest of their lives. After Mark has delivered, he is made a prisoner. Coriander and his boys walk out, and if we haven't gotten to Mark in a very few minutes, the time mechanism blows him, the girls, and the fifteenth floor to smithereens. But that's still the best chance of saving the children."

"I don't follow," Gus Brand said.

"He can't walk out with the children and Miss Horn and his soldiers, no matter how many. He can't get them all out and to safety—or to a waiting plane— without being spotted. You can't disguise those children. So Coriander knows he's going to die that way. Your sharpshooters don't miss. The only way he and his two or three friends are going to escape with their lives is to somehow mingle with the other hotel guests and walk away."

"How do they get off the fifteenth floor to mingle?" Brand asked.

"I don't know," Chambrun said. "But count on it, they've found a way. So they will wait for Mark to deliver whatever money is raised. They will hold him, locked away somewhere, walk out with the money. If we don't break in within minutes, Mark and the girls go boom."

"Why not just walk away?" Jim Priest asked. "Why blow up the hotel if they're free and clear?"

"Just in case their luck runs out," Chambrun said. "It will be a hole card for them if we catch up with them."

"You know something?" Jerry Dodd said. "If they can get out to 'mingle,' as you put it, we have no chance at all of spotting them. Coriander could walk into this office right now and we wouldn't know it was Coriander. We can forget that missing arm."

"Oh, by all means, let's forget the empty sleeve," Chambrun said. "So there you have it, Mr. Brand. If we buy his end-of-the-day plan, he walks out on us with whatever money's been raised, and luck will have to be on our side to save the hostages, which will include Mark. Coriander has only to get out of the hotel and he's lost in that mob of pickets and ghouls on the street. Has it occurred to you he can't let the children go? Even if he's worn that false face all the time they've been there, they're very bright girls. They will remember enough things about him, tricks of speech, physical mannerisms, even conversations overheard, to help us put an eventual finger on him."

"But don't we have to risk it?" Treadway asked. "We get ready to break in as soon as Mark has delivered the money and hope we get to the timing device before it sets off the explosives."

Brand seemed to be lost somewhere else. "One way or another, timing is everything," he said. "This is what I had in mind." He pointed at the blueprint with a yellow pencil. "The suite—Fifteen A—and the room next to it where the detonator is located are on the outside of the north wing—the east side looking toward the river. Across the street is an apartment building. The roof of that building comes just level with your fifteenth floor. The windows to the room where the detonator is located are here." He drew a circle on the blueprint. "Snipers on that roof, armed with rifles with telescopic sights, can see the man at the detonator as clearly as if they were just across the hall. He can't be just sitting there with a hand poised over a button hour after hour. He must light a cigarette, or get up and walk around the room to stretch his muscles, or involve himself with eating or drinking something. Maybe they change men. There has to be a moment when someone isn't poised directly over that detonator. When that moment comes, we open fire. Meanwhile we have men ready on the fire stairs outside the fifteenth-floor corridor. The moment the men on the roof open fire, we charge in. Properly timed, we get to the detonator before they can replace their dead men. We hopefully get to the children, in the confusion, before they do." He turned away from the blueprint. "I like this better than waiting to play it Coriander's way. His way the timing is his, he supplies the surprises. This way the timing is ours, the surprise element ours."

I liked it better, too. It didn't involve me!

"Your snipers are that good, Brand?" Treadway asked.

"With telescopic sights they can hit a dime at two hundred yards," Brand said. "We can drill that son-ofabitch at the detonator right in the eye."

"How do you coordinate with the men on the fire stairs?" Jim Priest asked.

"Coriander's friend isn't the only man with walk-ie-talkie equipment," Brand said. "From the moment the shots are fired to the moment we reach the detonator is a matter, literally, of seconds."

"How long will it take you to get set up?" Chambrun asked.

Brand glanced at his wrist watch. "Let's say an hour—just before noon."

"They'll be ordering something from Room Service, I'd guess, between twelve and one. They may be thrown off guard a little by the arrival of food. When the waiters are gone—" Chambrun was concerned for his people.

Brand looked around at all of us. Somebody was supposed to say "go."

Chambrun said it.

THREE

GUS BRAND WAS NOT a careless planner. I had a chance to watch him at work for a few minutes before I got an assignment from him that made me a part of what he referred to as his "game plan." It was, in effect, a military operation and I've seen men in charge of an attack in my time. Once the decision is made to "go," nothing matters except getting from point A to point B, losing as few men as possible in the process. Casualties are numbers and not human beings.

Gus Brand was something else again. He hated the gamble he was taking. He was genuinely concerned for the safety of innocent people, and particularly the safety of Elizabeth and Mariella Cleaves and Katherine Horn. Their lives depended on a kind of split-second efficiency.

People with rooms in the north wing on the sixteenth and fourteenth floors were to be kept away for the period of time between noon and the time when an "all clear" could be sounded. This in case Coriander's big explosion couldn't be prevented.

"We are guessing, without any proof, that Cleaves is the person on the outside who's making contact with Coriander," Brand said. Chambrun's office was the headquarters for the "game plan" and the cops and officials and our staff were waiting for instructions. "But for all we know there are others, God knows how many. That means we've got to get our men into position without anyone guessing what we're up to. I can't march twenty armed men through the lobby wearing bulletproof vests and attack helmets. We'd have a panic that way and the word gets to Coriander."

"Freight elevator," Chambrun said. "Your men can come in the service entrance, one or two at a time. You've got an hour to get them all into position."

Brand located the service entrance and the freight elevator on the blueprint. "That should do," he said. "There's no problem getting my sharpshooters on the roof of the adjoining building." He picked up one of the phones on Chambrun's desk and dialed an in-house number. He obviously had a man or men at a command post somewhere else in the hotel. "Plan A," he said in his quiet voice. He had worked out his scheme long before he proposed it to us. He glanced at his wrist watch. "The time now is eleven-O-six. Ready to move in exactly one hour. We'll hold then, however, if an order has been placed with Room Service and is in the process of being delivered. You will send in the attack squad through the service entrance and use the freight elevator. Say, two men at a time. Hold a minute." He covered the mouthpiece with his hand and looked at Jerry Dodd. "Do those men have to go through the kitchen area in full view of the staff there?"

"Kitchen area can be shut off," Jerry said. "The only persons who can't be avoided are the chief engineer and his assistant."

"You can have someone there to show our men the way, and make sure your engineer and his man aren't talking to someone on the walkie-talkie?"

"I'll cover it myself," Jerry said.

"Fine—with one of my men," Brand said. "I don't want a single step of the way covered by anyone outside my command. I'm going to have to take the rap if anything goes wrong." He smiled very faintly. "And the credit if it works." He turned back to the phone. "Dodd, the hotel security man, will meet you outside the hotel at the service entrance in five minutes?" He raised a questioning eyebrow to Jerry, who nodded and started out of the office. Brand put down the phone. "There are other angles to be covered." He fished a cigarette out of his pocket and lit it. "The joint is swarming with newspaper and media reporters. Every damned one of them is like a detective on the case. Anything that arouses the least suspicion will have them on our tails like a pack of bloodhounds."

"That should be easy," Chambrun said. "You haven't held your press conference yet this morning, have you, Mark?" I indicated no. "Well, call it for twelve o'clock. They all know you've been up to see Coriander. They're panting for that story. You should be able to keep them occupied in that special dining room for as long as is necessary."

I picked up the phone and called my office. I ordered the girls there to spread the word I'd meet with reporters at noon. That would be a nice, comfortable place to be when the shooting started.

"Finally," Brand said when I'd hung up, "not one word of this must leak to Cleaves, or Buck Ames, or Mrs. Cleaves." The tinted glasses turned my way. "I know you have a genuine sympathy for the lady, Haskell. But it will be easier for her to keep a secret she doesn't know than one she does. She might talk to her

father no matter what promises you extract from her.
I haven't written off Ames as Coriander's outside
contact. Mrs. Cleaves must think we're trying to meet
Coriander's demand for money and a safe flight to
Cuba.''

"I don't think she'd be reassured by what we're
doing," I said. "Seriously, how much chance do the
kids have?"

Brand glanced down at the blueprint. "It's about
forty feet from the door of the fire stairs to Fifteen A,
fifty to the door of 1507. If we knock out the man at
the detonator, we should have no problem there. But
the minute Coriander hears shooting, he'll know
what's up. If he turns on the girls then—" He let it ride
there.

"No one's going to open doors for you, you know,"
Chambrun said. "We can supply you with master
keys, but there are inside chain locks. It's going to take
time to break into any locked room."

"I have two men armed with bazookas," Brand
said. "We'll blow those doors open in seconds. The
children are down a corridor in the bedroom here." He
pointed at the blueprint. "They'll be safe from the
break-in. If Coriander isn't with the kids when it happens, we have a very good chance."

"If—for God's sake," I said. Those brave little girls
were very vivid to me.

"This plan or any other, the gamble is a big one,
Mark," Chambrun said. "This way we can hope that
surprise is working our way. The girls have almost no

chance in an open shoot-out on the way to a plane and Cuba."

"Or left behind to be blown to pieces by a timed explosion," Brand said. "It makes me ill just to think about it, but I'm certain this gives them their best chance—maybe the only one."

I wasn't protesting from strength, just a kind of sick anxiety for the children and for what the end result might do to Connie. You could talk and argue about it, but in less than an hour it would be NOW! A few agonizing minutes in time, no turning back, no second guessing, no alternatives once it began. All or nothing.

Feeling queasy and weak-kneed I went down the hall to my apartment. Somehow I had to see Connie, to bolster her courage without telling her what was really cooking.

Connie and Miss Ruysdale were sitting on the couch together, coffee, untouched and cold, on the table in front of them. Ruysdale had evidently busied herself trying to put the living room into some kind of order again. Connie looked at me from behind the black glasses, her lips parted in an unspoken question.

"Nothing yet," I said.

"No word from Buck?"

"Not yet."

"And Terrence?"

"Nothing." I tried to sound cheerful. "But there is more than five hours to the end of the business day."

Ruysdale stood up. "Can you stay with Mrs. Cleaves for a few minutes, Mark? I'd like very much to know if there is anything I can do for Mr. Chambrun."

I glanced at my watch. "I have a press conference in about twenty-five minutes," I said. "Take fifteen minutes if you want."

Connie leaned her head against the back of the couch. I imagined her eyes were shut. The door closed behind Ruysdale and we were alone together. I wanted to go to her, hold her, comfort her. I didn't. Instead I went to the kitchenette and poured a hot cup of coffee for myself and a fresh one for her.

"Why wouldn't he let me go up to the girls?" she asked. "What could it have cost him?" Her voice sounded lifeless.

"Perhaps he thought that down here you could help persuade people to meet his demands," I said.

"What could I persuade anyone to do that isn't being done?"

I wanted to say something absurd, like all the world loves a mother, but I didn't.

"What will I do if I don't get the children back?" she asked.

"You mustn't think that way," I said.

"You must have talked about it back there in the office—how much chance they've got."

"Mr. Brand thinks they have a very good chance," I said.

"If Coriander takes them off to Cuba?"

"It may not come to that—if he gets the money," I said.

"Without the children as hostages they won't let him go," she said. "Surely he knows that." She was facing reality. "You're not telling me the real truth, Mark. There is no chance for them, is there?"

"A good chance," I said. I sat down beside her on the couch and took her hands in mine. They were ice-cold. I had the crazy impulse to tell her, in spite of Brand's instructions, that in about forty-five minutes she might have the children back. She had just to hang on for that long. I came close, but I didn't.

"The very best trained men in the country are handling this," I said. "There couldn't be a better man in charge than Augustus Brand. He's not a crazy, trigger-happy kid. He's thinking about the children every step of the way."

"Oh, my God, Mark." She was suddenly in my arms, crying softly. I held her, kissing her forehead and her cheeks, muttering some inane words of comfort. When this was over, I told myself, no matter how it came out, I wasn't going to let her go. Not ever.

"You're very sweet, Mark," she whispered. "Very kind."

I was going to be a hell of a lot more than kind to her in the future.

There was a discreet knock on the door and I knew that Ruysdale was back. "Chin up," I said to Connie, like some sort of romantic idiot. I kissed her, very lightly, on the lips and went to the door. Ruysdale gave me an odd, faintly amused smile.

"Mr. Chambrun said to remind you that it's going on twelve o'clock," she said.

I explained to Connie that I had to meet with the reporters. I wished I could tell her that the next time I saw her we'd have all the answers, that however it came out I, Sir Mark the Glorious, would be standing by. I touched her cheek and got the hell out of there. My part of the plan, an important part, was about to begin. I was to keep the reporters occupied while Brand and his men gambled for the lives of the children and Katherine Horn.

It was ten minutes to noon.

At five minutes to twelve I walked into the private dining room and found a large crowd of men and women waiting for me. Cameras clicked. A few hundred yards away snipers were staring through their telescopic sights at the room where a man sat ready to blow up the hotel. I wished I'd asked Ruysdale whether an order had gone through to Room Service from 15 A. If it hadn't, the shooting would begin in about eight minutes. If it had, I might have to hang onto these people for quite a while.

I made a brief statement. Coriander had reduced his demands for the time being. He would accept the money and a safe flight to Cuba with his hostages. They could bargain for his other demands from there.

"Will the FBI buy that?" someone asked.

The questions came at me like machine-gun fire. I wanted them to keep coming, so I wasn't too direct with some answers. These people weren't dummies. They knew the past history of this kind of situation. That was all too fresh in all their minds—the shoot-out with the Hearst girl's friends in California, the jail break with hostages in Texas where two women were shot and killed rather than let the prisoners go free. A man from the *News* was particularly persistent.

"You have to be kidding," he said to me. "They're seriously considering supplying this Coriander with a plane and a safe getaway? They don't think that way."

"And can they raise the money?" someone else asked.

Round and round. And then the *News* man hit me with another tough one. "So you can only tell us what you're told to tell us," he said. "Let's try something else. Colin Andrews."

"You'll have to talk to Lieutenant Hardy about that," I said.

"Sure, sure. The police expect to make an early arrest. We don't like it very much, Haskell, when one of us is a target. It could get to be a habit."

"He was a nice guy," I said.

"He was a hell of a nice guy, working on a feature about Terrence Cleaves. What's the connection between these two cases, Haskell?"

"No connection that I know of."

"Andrews is having a drink with Martha Blodgett, who works for Cleaves. Connections all over the place."

"As a matter of fact Andrews and Miss Blodgett were having a drink in my apartment earlier in the evening. That doesn't connect me with it, does it?"

"You were also one of the people who answered the Blodgett girl's call for help. You were there. You saw it."

"Yes, I saw it."

"Is it true they were in the hay together when someone broke in and killed Colin?"

Now that was something that hadn't been mentioned in the first press releases on the story. Hardy had felt there was no advantage in exposing what would be thought of as a scandal for Martha. In the end, when he'd caught his man, it would probably have to be told. Right now Hardy was content to let the kidnapping be the big press story.

"You'll have to ask Lieutenant Hardy that question," I said.

"But you were there, Haskell!"

"It's Hardy's case," I said.

"Thanks for nothing," the *News* man said. "When we get around to writing the truth, I'll personally take pleasure in letting the public know what kind of a joint the Beaumont really is."

I was about to try to cool him off when I saw Johnny Thacker, the day bell captain, waving frantically at me from the back of the room. I looked at my watch. It was twenty past twelve. I felt my heart jam against my ribs. It could all be over up on the fifteenth floor. I excused myself, got a yowl of protest, and elbowed my way through the crowd to Johnny.

"You're wanted upstairs on the double. Boss's office. Drop everything and run is the word," Johnny said.

The stairway was quicker than waiting for an elevator. I took it, two steps at a time, and I hit Chambrun's office out of breath. The Assistant Commissioner, Jim Priest, and Captain Valentine were with the boss. I really didn't want to hear how it had worked out. I had a premonition that it had all gone very wrong.

Chambrun, looking like that hanging judge I've mentioned in connection with him, had the phone to his ear, but he wasn't talking. Only when I came in did he speak.

"He's here now," he said, and held the phone out to me.

My mouth felt dry. "The children?" I asked.

Chambrun didn't say anything. He just held the phone for me to take.

I managed to say, "Mark Haskell here."

"Brand," the FBI man said. "Do you have the blueprint there in front of you on the desk?"

"Yes."

"Count the windows down from the closed end of the corridor to the windows in the bedroom where the children are being kept."

I checked them off. "Eight windows, and then the two windows in the bedroom where the children are."

"Were," Brand said.

"Oh, no," I said. "You mean—?"

"There's nobody in that room. Now count on till you come to the windows in 1507 where the detonator is."

"Two windows in the other bedroom in the suite— Fifteen A. A frosted window in the bathroom. Then two windows in 1507."

"My men on the roof across the way," Brand said in a voice that sounded strained, "looking through their telescopic sights, can see into those rooms as clearly as if they were just outside the windows. There's nobody visible in the bedrooms of the suite. There's nobody in 1507. There is no detonator in 1507. Venetian blinds are drawn on every other window on the corridor. You can't have been wrong about the rooms?"

"Not a chance."

"The sonofabitch is laughing at us," Brand said. "He knows or guessed what we planned."

"You're not going in?" I asked him.

"How can we if he's expecting us and we don't know where the children are, or where they've placed the detonator? The factor of surprise has changed hands. Put Chambrun on."

I handed the phone to Chambrun. He listened and then put down the phone without speaking a word. He looked around at us.

"He's got us licked and hung out to dry," he said.

I'd never heard him admit defeat before.

BRAND JOINED US in the office a few moments later. His attack force was still grouped on the fire stairs outside 15 North, on the landing and on the flights up and down, waiting for instructions.

"I don't suppose Coriander had to be a genius to anticipate what we might try. He figured out his weak spot just the way we figured it, only he moved faster. He also knows now that we have no intention of letting him walk out of here, with or without his hostages, with or without some ransom money."

"So what does he do next?" Jim Priest asked.

Brand was bending over the blueprint on the desk. "Look, Mr. Chambrun," he said. "You said earlier on that you were certain Coriander had some kind of escape route. Show me, on this floor plan, how it's possible. We have the fire stairs blocked. He can't get around to the west wing without our seeing him go. I promise you he can't just shoot his way out, army against army. We can reinforce our men without limitation. He's only got however many men there are up on fifteen. There's no way to add to them."

"There are a couple of thousand people outside the hotel," Priest said.

"And I'd swear only a handful of them can possibly be organized," Brand said. "The rest of them are just sightseers. Show me his way out, Chambrun."

Chambrun wasn't looking at the blueprint. His eyes were buried deep in their pouches and he was concentrated on something far away in time and space.

"The only possible way is by the elevators or the elevator shafts," Brand said. "Now the elevators are manned by security, and nothing is going to force them to stop at Fifteen. We can cut off the power for all the elevators in the hotel on a moment's notice. I talked to your engineer in the basement. He's standing by just in case."

"A human fly," Chambrun said in a faraway voice. He wasn't being serious, I knew. "Walk down the outside of the building—or up to the roof. Walk down or up the inside of the elevator shaft."

"Go ahead, kid around," Brand said angrily. "We may not have planned to stop him walking up or down the outside walls of the building. But the elevator shaft is impossible. He's got to get to it, and he can't even show his face—or his false face—in the fifteenth-floor corridor without my men seeing him."

"And he knows that as well as you do," Chambrun said, still far away. "You've got him backed into a corner. But bear in mind, Mr. Brand, he must have known from the beginning that's exactly how it would be. So I tell you, he has a way out."

"Where? How, god damn it?"

"He begins to work on us another way," Jim Priest suggested. "Piece-by-piece mutilation of the children until we cry for mercy."

"I hope you're wrong, Jim," Chambrun said. "I think he will wait for whatever money we get up for him, and then he will walk away with it."

I thought for a moment Brand was going to attack Chambrun physically. "Will you stop jabbering and tell me how?"

"Magic. Basic principles of the magic trick," Chambrun said. "We concentrate on the elevators, the fire stairs, the outside of the building, if you like, and while our attention is focused on those points, he walks away."

"A helicopter from the roof," Jim Priest suggested.

"He can't get up to the roof!" Brand literally shouted. He brought his fist down on the desk so hard that Chambrun's tiny coffee cup jumped. "He can't 'walk away'!"

"Figure of speech," Chambrun said. He looked at the frustrated FBI man and the corners of his mouth twitched with a smile he fought to control. "He flies out the window. He has learned the secret of the Invisible Man. 'Down the drain' he said about Horween."

"Will you stop talking that kind of crap?" Brand said. "Human lives, your building; those are the stakes."

"Have we given up on the possibility that Cleaves is Coriander?" Priest asked. "He'll walk away because he isn't there."

"But there are people there we know about," Brand said. "The man in the false face and wig and the empty sleeve. We know he's there. At least two men Mark saw wearing stocking masks. You saw all three of those men at the same time, together, on your second visit. No?"

"Yes," I said.

"He leaves them to be mowed down or blown up, along with the hostages?" Brand said.

"I think they 'walk away,' too," Chambrun said. "Please, Mr. Brand, I'm not trying to irritate you. It's just a conviction of mine. I've never believed in the Army For Justice. If it exists, Coriander is just using it for his personal gain. The money is everything. I think he always meant to settle for the money. I think he'll take a very great deal less than his two hundred and fifty million. I think he and his handful of henchmen will take it and 'walk away' with it. I haven't figured out how, but it's the only thing that makes any sense. So I, personally, have to assume that's the way it's planned. They'll frighten us with threats, but actually they'll just walk away with a fortune, laughing at us."

"Well, I'll make you a promise, Chambrun. He won't 'walk away.' No chance. No way."

I guess it won't be too hard for anyone to guess that I was thinking about myself. If money was to be delivered to Coriander, I was going to have to be the messenger. Since it couldn't be what he'd asked for, it looked as if I would join Elizabeth and Mariella and Katherine Horn for the payoff. It was a pretty scary prospect. Chambrun must have read my mind, because after Brand and the others had left the office to shore up their defenses, he spoke to me with something like paternal affection.

"I don't ask you to go back up there when the time comes," he said.

"All that stuff about flying out the window," I said. "What do you really think?"

"I really think he has a careful plan for escape," Chambrun said.

"But Brand is right. There is no way," I said.

"Brand is wrong," he said, his face hardening. "There has to be a way." He reached for a cigarette in the box on his desk. "Cleaves and Buck Ames will show up with what will look like a small fortune to you and me. It will be far short of Coriander's demand." He lit his cigarette. "Coriander will have to be persuaded to accept it. My guess is that he will. For all his fancy talk, he's a realist. I have a feeling that he knows, almost to the penny, what Cleaves and Buck can raise. I don't think he'll take too much time to argue about it. But I don't think that you—or whoever takes him the money—will be allowed to simply deliver and come back downstairs. I think the messenger will be kept as a hostage."

"I'll go," I said. "I promised those kids I'd be back."

"Don't be a sentimental ass," he said.

"You haven't seen them," I said. "You don't know how much they mean to Connie."

"So let me mention something to you that I didn't say to Brand, because he knows it." Chambrun put out the cigarette on which he'd only taken a couple of drags. "Coriander's explosives are carefully placed. Only he knows where they are all located. If they are all set off at once, the fire stairs will go and Brand's men will be buried under rubble or blown to pieces. Everybody on Fifteen except those who know how to protect themselves when the blast comes will be blown to pieces."

"Protect themselves?" I asked.

"Some room, probably one closest to the fire stairs, will not have been mined. In the terrible confusion that could follow the blast Coriander and his boys could, quite literally, walk out."

"To the floor below or the floor below that," I said. "But then Brand's reserves will have every hallway, stairway, exit, blocked. If Coriander is so smart, he'll know that, too."

"That's why I think it's going to be very much less obvious, very much simpler. But I repeat, Mark, you don't have to run the risk. I couldn't ask you to."

"I'll go," I said, feeling heroic.

FOUR

TIME MOVED ON with frightening speed as far as I was concerned. The end of the business day was, I took it, five o'clock. Coriander might give us a little more than that, assuming that Cleaves and Buck Ames would be working at the money raising till the very last minute.

Actually it was about four o'clock when Terrence Cleaves checked into Chambrun's office. He was carrying a fairly large black suitcase. He looked washed up. Brand and Jim Priest were with us in the office.

"It's pitifully small in relation to his demands," he said, as he put the suitcase down beside Chambrun's desk. "A million, three hundred thousand dollars. Everything I own in the world is pledged against it." His mouth twisted into a bitter smile. "Everything I own now or will ever own. I've heard enough sympathy to drown in, and a lot of bloody talk about law and order. But I come up with pitifully less than we need." He drew a deep breath. "If you'll excuse me, I need to go to the little boy's room."

"Mr. Cleaves!" Brand said.

"Yes?"

"Before you go, I have to ask you to submit to a body search."

Cleaves looked at the FBI man as though he didn't believe what he'd heard.

"This office isn't bugged," Brand said, "yet Coriander knows everything that goes on here. We have to believe that someone on the inside is communicating with some sort of walkie-talkie mechanism. If you'll stand by the wall there, put your hands against it, spread your legs."

"You have to be joking," Cleaves said.

"Far from it, Mr. Cleaves."

"I'm supposed to be in cahoots with Coriander?"

"You could be," Brand said.

"How utterly absurd," Cleaves said. But he assumed the attitude, and Brand frisked him very thoroughly. He came up with nothing.

"Thank you, Mr. Cleaves."

Cleaves straightened up and he surveyed all of us with angry eyes. "Do you honestly think I could be in on a plan to hurt my own children?"

"Our faith in you would be strengthened if we knew what it is your wife has on you, Mr. Cleaves," Chambrun said. "It might help us to understand why Colin Andrews was murdered. We'd understand why your wife was beaten, tied up while you searched Mark's apartment."

"You miserable prick!" Cleaves said, his voice shaken. "My private life is none of your concern, nor does it have anything to do with Coriander and my children." He turned and walked through into the dressing room and the john.

"He could easily have gotten rid of any kind of communicating device before he came back here," Brand said. He shook his head. "Unless Buck Ames comes up with something really substantial, Coriander isn't going to deal with us."

"You can live very comfortably for a long time on something more than a million and a quarter," Chambrun said.

"Coriander has bigger dreams," Brand said.

Chambrun's eyes were narrowed. "Maybe," he said.

AT A QUARTER PAST FOUR Buck Ames appeared carrying a suitcase and a black attaché case. He had come up with three million dollars in cash. He laughed when Brand asked him to submit to a body search, submitted to it without argument. He was clean. He, too, could have gotten rid of anything he'd been carrying earlier.

We sat silent, waiting for word from the fifteenth floor. Time seemed to drag, now. At about a quarter to five Captain Valentine and the Assistant Commissioner checked in. Treadway had arranged for a hundred cops to hold back the street crowds and block every entrance and exit from the hotel.

"Just on the chance that Chambrun is right," Brand said, "and Coriander plans to walk out, I don't want any luggage taken out of the hotel without its being searched. You can't carry four million dollars in your watch pocket or a woman's handbag." He looked at the suitcases and the attaché case stacked by Chambrun's desk. "We don't know what Coriander looks like, but we know he can't be traveling light."

Word was conveyed to Jerry Dodd's office.

And we waited.

At twenty minutes past five the red light blinked on Chambrun's phone. He switched on the squawk box and answered.

"Is the war cabinet assembled, Mr. Chambrun?" Coriander's sardonic voice came through the speaker.

"We're listening," Chambrun said.

"What kind of proposition do you have for me?"

"I'll let Mr. Brand talk to you," Chambrun said.

Coriander chuckled. "I'm rather disappointed in Mr. Brand," he said. "I know the FBI type of mind so well. Agreements and promises aren't worth anything. Did you imagine, Mr. Brand, that I wouldn't be ready for your sharpshooters and your army? I mean, really. A child could have foreseen that kind of tactics."

"I'll let you have it straight," Brand said. "We have four million three hundred thousand dollars in cash for you here in this office."

"Dear me, that's rather far short of my demands and, I might add, needs. I'm afraid you are forcing me to the unpleasant business of making it quite clear to you that I'm not joking. It's too bad that Elizabeth and Mariella have to pay for your lack of cooperation."

"Coriander, listen!" Buck Ames cried out. "This is Buck Ames. I swear to you we have tapped every possible source for money. Within the business day, you said. If there was more time, perhaps governments might untrack themselves for more. You know as well as I do that's not an instant possibility. You want to carve someone up, let me take the place of the girls!"

"You can take me, too!" Cleaves said in a shaken voice.

"Aren't you moved by all that heroism, Coriander?" Chambrun said. I looked at him because his voice had taken on a note of mockery that matched Coriander's. "Suppose we talk facts. Four and a quarter million dollars plus is a pretty handsome take. You see, I know what you're going to do."

"Oh? What am I going to do?"

"You're going to take the money after torturing the children's parents and grandfather with threats against them. You are going to hold Mark Haskell as hostage when he brings you the money. You plan to walk away, assuring us that if we try to break in, it will set off your bombs. You will tell us that when you are safe you will telephone us with directions on how to deactivate the bombs. That's what you're going to do."

Again the amused chuckle. "You're a very interesting antagonist, Chambrun. What about the plane and safe passage to Cuba?"

"You wouldn't dream of taking a plane if we had a fleet of them waiting for you," Chambrun said. "You'd never expose yourself to FBI sharpshooters. You know they'd be waiting, even if you have the children with you. You say you know the FBI mind, so you know that's how it will be."

"And how am I supposed to leave the hotel with the money, with Brand's men everywhere, with half the New York City police force patrolling outside and inside?" Coriander asked.

"I wish I knew the answer to that," Chambrun said. "But I know there is a way, or you wouldn't have played your hand the way you have."

"Can't you guess?" Coriander asked, laughter still near the surface.

"I've made a dozen guesses, but none of them quite makes sense."

The amusement was suddenly gone from Coriander's voice. "You've made a number of mistakes, gentlemen," he said. "You sent that idiot Horween up here to try to outplay me. You must be satisfied by the result that I mean business. You've tried to stage a surprise attack which, as I've said, a child could have foreseen. You would be well advised not to make any more errors of commission."

"I'm listening," Chambrun said.

"The money is ridiculously inadequate, but I believe it's probably the maximum that Cleaves and Ames could raise. I need to discuss it with my lieutenants. If they agree to accept that pitiful fraction of what we want, I will then have instructions for you. I'll call back in about fifteen minutes."

The phone clicked off.

"He didn't say anything about political prisoners or generals to be tried for crimes," Buck Ames said.

"I've said from the start that all he cared about was money," Chambrun said. "The rest was window dressing to gain public support. I don't believe there is an Army For Justice; just a handful of very clever criminals. He's got to move while all your men are on the alert, Brand, and while the police are patrolling."

"I don't get it," Brand said.

"Because that's part of his way out," Chambrun said. "Orderly confusion is part of his magic trick."

"You let him go, with the girls, until he's away and safe?" Cleaves asked.

"I don't think he will take the girls anywhere," Chambrun said. "They'll be more use to him here, waiting to be blown up if we don't follow his instructions."

"If he shows his face, he's a dead man, hostages or no hostages," Brand said.

"Shows what face, Mr. Brand?" Chambrun asked. "That's the most fascinating part of it all. What face?"

We waited. Brand made contact with various check points in the hotel. His men were in place. He was satisfied that escape was impossible, but somehow Chambrun had shaken his absolute certainty.

"I've been thinking of one thing," Brand said. "Suppose you're right and he plans to 'walk away,' leaving the bombs set to go off if we break in before he tells us we can. That detonator is probably connected to a floor plug or a light fixture. There must be a master switch that will turn off all the power in the hotel. We throw the switch and go in. Unless he's left armed men behind him—"

"And how would they hope to get away?" Chambrun asked. "I think we can forget the thought that this is a great moral cause with Coriander some sort of messiah. They are crooks, and they all mean to survive. As for the detonator, you can bet your life that it's battery-operated. The first thing he would expect us to think of, after he'd shown Mark the detonator, would be to turn off the current."

"There can be some sort of trip wire that will set off the explosives the minute we open the fire stairs door," Captain Valentine said.

"But not until Coriander and his lieutenants, as he calls them, are safe," Chambrun said. "He wants to live and enjoy the money."

We talked round and round the problem, getting nowhere, it seemed to me. And then the red light blinked on Chambrun's phone again. Coriander was back.

"We have decided to go with the money you've raised," he said. No amusement this time.

"I rather imagined you would," Chambrun said.

"It's a pity to have gone to so much trouble for so little return," Coriander said, "but we've made our choice. Now listen very carefully, because I don't intend to repeat, and you won't have Haskell to relay instructions.''

"Go ahead.''

You can be damned sure I was listening.

"How is the money packed?"

"Two suitcases and an attaché case.''

"Have Haskell bring them up. When he gets here, if he behaves himself and doesn't try any heroics, he will be trussed up like the proverbial Christmas goose and left in one of the rooms on this floor. The other hostages, the children and Miss Horn, will be handled in the same fashion. My lieutenants and I will leave, and when we are safely away, I will phone you instructions on how to deactivate the explosives. If you try to go in before you get word from me, you will set off the explosives yourself. The responsibility will be yours. Understood?"

"Quite clear," Chambrun said.

"Does the FBI understand?"

"I understand," Brand said.

"Send Haskell now," Coriander said, and cut the connection.

"It doesn't make sense," Brand said. "There isn't a bat-crack for them to slip through.''

"We have no choice but to play it his way," Chambrun said. He turned to me. "I still say I can't ask you to do this, Mark."

"I'll go," I said.

He came over and put his hand on my shoulder. "If I didn't think you'll almost certainly be safe, I'd prevent your going," he said.

"Almost certainly" weren't exactly the most encouraging words I'd ever heard.

"I'm not permitting an elevator to stop at Fifteen," Brand said. "Coriander may have some crazy idea of getting on the car when you get off and trying that way out. You'll have to take the bags up to Sixteen and walk down. My men are crowded on the fire stairs, but they'll know you're coming."

I picked up the bags. Four million dollars turned out to be heavy as hell. Brand agreed to carry one of the bags to the elevator.

As we reached the door of the office, I heard Cleaves say, "Good luck and God bless."

Brand and I went down the hall to the elevator. Just as we got there, I found myself wondering about going in from the fire stairs. It could blow up the joint.

"Let's hope not," Brand said. "I think he wants the money too badly."

There was an operator and one of Jerry's men on the elevator. I said goodbye to Brand. I felt as though I was going to the moon. The elevator whished up far too fast to suit me. Outside the door to the fire stairs on Sixteen two of Brand's men were waiting for me. They looked as if they were going to the moon, too: thick bulletproof vests, their faces hidden by the bulletproof glass windows in their attack helmets. We didn't say anything to each other beyond a muttered hello. They helped me with the bags. I didn't have to do anything but wedge my way through and past a couple of dozen other men from Mars who were crowded on the stairway, armed with rifles and machine pistols.

We came to a stop outside the fifteenth-floor door that would open into the corridor beyond. The last thing I wanted to do was open that door, because it was the last thing I might ever do. I put my hands on the door handle, closed my eyes, and opened the door. Nothing happened. The armed men handed the suitcases in and closed the door. I was on 15 North, as deserted as it had been on my earlier visits. I dragged the suitcases down to the door of 15 A. I put them down and knocked.

One of the stocking-masked men opened the door. He took one of the bags from me and I carried the other and the attaché case into the living room. Coriander and the other stocking-masked guy were there, Coriander sitting on the edge of the table, swinging a leg the way he'd done the last time I was there. The false face was the same, the wig the same, the empty sleeve the same.

"Forgive us if we examine the contents, Haskell," he said. "I shouldn't like to get away and discover that the clever Mr. Chambrun had sent us the Sunday *Times* or a few Manhattan telephone books."

One of the stocking masks opened the bags while the other stood a few feet away, a machine pistol aimed casually at my breastbone. Coriander watched the counting process. It would have taken forever to count all the bills, but they seemed satisfied that it was all money.

"You understand that we're going to have to immobilize you, Haskell," Coriander said.

"Let me see the children first," I said. "I promised them I'd be back."

"An admirable sentiment," Coriander said, "but I'm afraid there isn't time. Be good enough to sit down in that armchair."

I sat down and one of the stocking masks went to work on me. Each of my ankles was taped to a leg of the chair. My hands were taped to the arms. He faced me with a wide strip in his hands that was obviously going over my mouth.

"Don't feel you're getting special treatment," Coriander said. "The children and Miss Horn are already in the same situation. If Chambrun and Brand obey instructions, you'll all be having a midnight supper together."

Six hours of being a Christmas goose, I thought. "There just isn't any way out for you," I said, "unless, as Chambrun suggested, you can make yourself invisible."

He laughed. "An interesting idea," he said. He gestured to Stocking Mask, who slapped the adhesive over my mouth. "It's been a pleasure dealing with you, Haskell."

He and the two men carried the bags and the attaché case out into the hall and closed the door.

I was alone, unable to move much more than to wiggle my behind on the chair seat. The silence in that soundproofed room was so loud I think I would have screamed if my mouth hadn't been taped shut.

IT WASN'T UNTIL sometime afterwards that I knew what happened in Chambrun's office. Chambrun and Brand and Priest and the others waited, and presently one of Brand's men checked with him. I'd made it onto the fifteenth floor.

After a while Buck Ames exploded. "What the hell do we do, just sit here and wait for that bastard to phone us from Kalamazoo?"

Chambrun glanced at his watch. "I think we might as well go up and release the hostages," he said.

Brand stared at him. "We're to wait till he phones."

"He won't phone," Chambrun said. "He really doesn't expect us to wait very long."

"You can't risk it," Cleaves said. "The girls—"

"Coriander is gone," Chambrun said. His eyes were so bright, Brand told me afterwards, that he had to look away. "Gone forever."

"Impossible," Brand said.

"Not only possible but accomplished," Chambrun said. "I think it will be quite safe to go up and in."

"And pull the trigger on the bombs!" Cleaves said.

"There won't be any explosion," Chambrun said.

"How do you know?"

"Because I finally know the way Coriander could 'walk away,'" Chambrun said.

IF I'D KNOWN that Chambrun and Brand were planning to invade the fifteenth floor, I might just have quietly passed out. I hadn't a doubt in my mind that Coriander had left things set up so that the place would be blown up to hell and gone if anyone tried to attack.

It wasn't, I learned later, anything like an attack. Chambrun commandeered an elevator, and over the protests of Cleaves and Buck Ames, and accompanied by Gus Brand, who had apparently decided to put himself in Chambrun's hands, and Jerry Dodd, who would have walked into the lion's den if Chambrun had asked it, they went directly to 15.

Chambrun suggested that Brand let his men in from the stairway. No need to bother looking for a trip wire, Chambrun assured the FBI man. Brand looked anyway, found nothing, and the men from Mars came in off the fire stairs, guns at the ready.

"Find that detonator!" Brand ordered. "Search every room on this floor."

Chambrun walked casually down the hall to the door of 15 A, unlocked it with a pass key, and walked in.

I nearly fainted when I saw him. Brand was just behind him along with two men in attack helmets waving guns. Chambrun came over to me, smiling.

"This is going to hurt a little," he said, and ripped the adhesive off my mouth before I realized what he was talking about.

"Coriander phoned you so soon?"

"No phone call," Chambrun said, working on my wrists and ankles.

"You took a chance on the bombs exploding?"

"Not really a chance," Chambrun said. "There. Stand up and stretch your legs."

"The children!" I said.

We found them two rooms down the hall along with Katherine Horn. They were trussed up the same way I'd been. Chambrun and I got them free. The two girls were laughing and crying. Katherine Horn looked as if she'd lived through some kind of nightmare.

But the big surprise happened a moment later. Two of the armed FBI agents came into the room where we were with the children, and walking between them, a stubble of red beard shadowing his face, was Douglas Horween, supposedly dead. He was wearing a sports shirt, a pair of summer-weight slacks that looked slept in, and loafers on his feet.

"I thought you'd never come," he said to us, "and most of the time I hoped you wouldn't. That bastard was crazy enough to blow us all to hell. I've been tied up down the hall since yesterday."

"He told us he'd killed you," Brand said. "We had the clothes you were wearing when you came up here posing as a waiter. Your blood was apparently on them."

Horween rolled back a shirt sleeve. "They carved me up to get that blood," he said, revealing a deep cut on his arm. "He wanted you to be sure he meant business. I imagined he had another plan for me later if he came to a showdown. Have you got him?"

We didn't have him. We had his false face and the fright wig and the red bathrobe, all discarded in a room—1511—where the detonator was now placed. The detonator wasn't hooked up to anything. Captain Valentine and his bomb experts were gathering up the explosive charges all along the hallway and in the rooms. Coriander was gone. The two stocking-masked men were gone. The two suitcases and the attaché case that had well over four million dollars were in 1511, empty. Horween and the two girls and Miss Horn and I had been the only people left on the fifteenth floor when Chambrun and Brand and the men from Mars had come in. Brand was in a state. Nobody had left the fifteenth floor by the fire stairs or by the elevators in the north and west wings, or by the freight elevators. But three men had gone, plus heavy luggage that couldn't be concealed.

Horween requested permission to go to 1507, which had been his room before Coriander took over. He'd like to get clean clothes, a shower, a shave. Brand was sorry. No one was to go into any of the rooms until the entire fifteenth floor was dusted for fingerprints from one end to the other.

"As I recall, you have clothes in a locker in the waiters' quarters at Room Service," Chambrun said.

"Mark or I can supply you with a shower and shaving equipment."

"Of course, I'd forgotten," Horween said.

"Coriander must have stripped you naked," Chambrun said. "He sent us everything you were wearing as Fritz Schindler."

"Naked as the day I was born," Horween said with a bitter smile. "They got me these things out of my room."

"After drawing blood to fool us," Chambrun said.

"After that, yes," Horween said. "I—I owe you an apology, Chambrun. I damn near got myself killed by not obeying your orders."

"I'm sure Mr. Brand has a lot of questions to ask all of you," Chambrun said, looking around at the girls and Katherine Horn. "I'm sure the children's parents and their grandfather are beside themselves at this moment. I suggest we join them in my office."

The reunion of the children with their parents and old Buck Ames was a moving thing to watch—Connie, on her knees, hugging and kissing them both; Cleaves, standing at a distance, his face working, waiting his turn to welcome them home; Buck Ames, pounding anyone who came near him on the back, announcing this was the happiest goddam moment of his whole life. Horween retired to the boss's dressing room after being greeted with surprise and relief. A waiter from Room Service delivered the clothes he'd left there.

Jerry Dodd had come down from Fifteen with Chambrun. I'd gone down first with the kids and Katherine Horn. Jerry looked grimly content about something. Evidently Chambrun had told him something that none of the rest of us knew.

Finally, just as Horween was emerging from the dressing room, shaved, wearing clean clothes, his bright red hair damp from a shower, Brand rejoined us. He was an angry man.

"All right, Mr. Chambrun, I've followed your lead up to now," he said. "Now I want explanations. Nobody left the fifteenth floor, but three men are gone. Three men, the contents of two heavy suitcases, and an attaché case."

"Have you counted noses?" Chambrun asked. He was sitting at his desk, the cat who'd swallowed the canary, lighting a cigarette as Miss Ruysdale brought him a cup of his beloved Turkish coffee.

"What noses? What do you mean, counted noses?"

"Do you know how many men you had wearing those bulky vests and attack helmets?"

"Twenty on the north side, ten more on the west side," Brand said.

"I suggest that in the confusion they were augmented by at least two men, dressed exactly like them, who eventually left Fifteen without anyone questioning them. They were probably a little fatter than the others because they had four million dollars in money hidden under those bulletproof vests. Walked out, as I told you they would. You'll find the vests and the attack helmets discarded in a broom closet somewhere."

"You knew it was going to happen and you let it happen right under our noses?" Brand said, his voice shaken with anger.

"I wasn't particularly interested in those two men," Chambrun said. "To have tried to stop them would have cost us lives. I was only really concerned about Coriander and the money. The money had to be passed to someone who could, when the excitement is all over, carry it out in luggage. Carried out by one of Coriander's outside contacts."

I found myself looking at Cleaves, the Coldstream Guardsman. God knows he had needed money.

"I suppose you know who that outside contact is?" Brand said.

"I'll make a guess—a little later," Chambrun said. He looked at Horween. "I find myself fascinated by your extraordinary red hair, Mr. Horween. As a child were you ever, by any chance, called 'Carrot Top'?"

Horween grinned. "My father's pet name for me," he said. "How did you know?"

"I looked up the word 'coriander' in the dictionary," Chambrun said. "'A plant of the carrot family, with a strong-smelling seedlike fruit used in flavoring foods and in medications.' Shall we stop playing games?"

"Games?" Horween's eyes had narrowed and his face suddenly looked marble-hard.

"An expert at disguises," Chambrun said, sipping at his coffee. "I don't think you intended to run off with the money to some country from which you couldn't be extradited. I think you meant to spend it here, in your own world, and to live happily ever after with the lady of your choice."

"I simply don't know what you're talking about," Horween said.

"Colonel Coriander—Carrot Top," Chambrun said. "Interesting how we go back to childhood associations when we start to play charades."

"Are you suggesting," Horween asked in a low voice, "that I am Coriander?"

"I'm not suggesting it; I know it," Chambrun said. "If I had been wrong, I would be dead at this moment, and so would the children and Miss Horn and you and God knows how many of Brand's men." He glanced at Brand. "There was no way out, my friend. You proved that to your own satisfaction. But there had to be a way out. Horween, a master of disguise, becomes Fritz Schindler, a room service waiter, and disobeys our orders. He goes up with food and drink for Fifteen A. Why? Because he had to get up there to command the operation. You see, he had an alibi for when the kidnapping took place. He was with Mr. Cleaves at the United Nations. That seemed to prove he wasn't the kidnapper. So now he must join his collaborators who are holding the children and Miss Horn. Fritz Schindler had access. Horween took his place and got where he had to be. The case of Horween is closed when we get Schindler's bloodied clothes."

"But," I said in a very small voice. "But I first talked to Coriander while Horween was still with Cleaves at the U.N."

"You talked to a man in a false face, with a fright wig and an empty sleeve. Ten different men could have assumed that outrageous disguise and they would have all seemed like one and the same man. The first Coriander you talked to was not Horween. The other times it was."

"I think I've had about enough of this nonsense," Horween said. He started for the office door.

"Not just yet, friend," Brand said. He was blocking the way. "What made you sure Coriander was Horween, Chambrun?"

"You have to believe what you know to be facts,"
Chambrun said. "We knew that no one had gone up
to Fifteen or left it except the room service waiters,
Horween disguised as one of them, and Mark. No one
else had come or gone. Fact. You very efficiently covered every possible avenue of escape. No way out.
Fact. But there had to be a way out. So the only way
was after a break-in by your men. Fact. So there
wouldn't be an explosion because Coriander was still
on the fifteenth floor. So it was safe to go in. Some of
the people in Coriander's group would mingle with the
attack squad. They'd know how your men would be
equipped because that kind of business has been Horween's profession. But Horween wouldn't leave that
way, because he wants to live openly and publicly in
his world with a tidy fortune, even after he splits with
his helpers, to provide all the luxuries of life. So, I
reasoned, Coriander would be found—with a story to
tell of how he, too, had been a hostage. He would walk
away with us. Now he couldn't walk out into the open
unless he had an ironclad alibi for the kidnapping. So
it had to be Horween. Fact. Enough fact, Mr.
Brand?"

"Not quite," Brand said. "We have a murder that
wasn't a fake on our hands. We have an accomplice
who was in this office when we gave Mark instructions before his third visit to Fifteen A. We have a lot
of double talk about something Mrs. Cleaves had on
her husband, and something Cleaves had on Buck
Ames."

Chambrun smiled at him. "I would have to guess
about the double talk," he said. "Maybe the time has
come for Mr. Cleaves to come clean with us. But as to
the accomplice, I don't have to guess. Jerry?"

Jerry Dodd held out his hand. In it was a small transistor type walkie-talkie gadget. "While Mrs. Cleaves was getting her children, I took this out of her handbag," he said.

Connie! I couldn't believe it. I looked at her where she was sitting with the children huddled close to her. I saw her snatch at the handbag on the table beside her and open it. The black glasses hid most of her expression except for her mouth, which had become a straight, hard slit.

"Mrs. Cleaves also went into the dressing room at the time when someone had to have been in touch with Coriander," Chambrun said.

"Baby! Oh, my God," Buck Ames said.

What happened then was too fast and too startling for anyone to anticipate. Connie stood up and she took something out of her bag and tossed it to Horween. It was a very serviceable-looking Police Special. Horween covered us with it.

"All right, love," he said. "You wait for me in the outer office. Don't move, any of you. I am a notoriously good shot with this kind of weapon, and at this distance I can make holes right between your eyes. I think to guarantee our safe departure I will take you, Miss Ruysdale, as a hostage and a shield. Everyone seems so fond of you. I'm sure Mr. Chambrun wouldn't want you hurt. Step over in front of me, please, pausing on the way to relieve Mr. Brand of his gun." It was Coriander's mocking voice coming out of Horween's mouth.

"Stay where you are, Ruysdale," Chambrun said. He got up from his desk and started to move toward Horween.

"I warn you, Chambrun, one more step and the legendary host of the Beaumont will be a dead legend."

Chambrun kept walking, slowly, quite steadily toward Horween.

"Don't, Pierre!" Miss Ruysdale cried out.

I tried to move and found I was frozen. Chambrun had a strange smile on his face. I saw Horween's finger tighten on the trigger—and nothing but an empty click happened as he began to pull it.

At the same instant Terrence Cleaves lunged at Horween from the side. I suspect Horween was a very tough fighter, and he was younger and physically stronger than Cleaves, but he was momentarily shocked by the failure of the gun to fire. Cleaves had him by the throat with his left hand, smashing at him with his right. They went down on the rug and I saw the gun rise and fall—twice. Cleaves had it and he was pounding at Horween's skull with the butt. Brand and Jerry pulled Cleaves off an unconscious and bloody Horween.

"You must be crazy, Chambrun," Buck Ames said. "Except for the luck of the gun misfiring—"

Jerry Dodd, still holding onto a charged-up Cleaves, grinned at the Buccaneer. "I took time to unload it when I was going through Mrs. Cleaves's purse," he said.

Chambrun looked at Miss Ruysdale. "So I wasn't as heroic as I tried to make myself look," he said.

And then Connie was back in the room, down on the floor beside Horween, cradling his bloody head in her lap, crooning over him.

THE REST CAME OUT in bits and pieces after the children had been taken away by Miss Horn and their grandfather, after Horween had been carried down to the Beaumont's hospital, guarded by Jerry and a couple of Brand's men, and after Connie had been taken away in handcuffs to God knows where.

Lieutenant Hardy, the homicide man, appeared, sent for by Chambrun. It was Terrence Cleaves, his rigid control broken, who gave us answers, choking over the words from time to time.

His world had fallen apart some four years ago when he found that his wife was involved in a passionate love affair with Horween—Horween, the glamorous adventurer, still working as an agent for the British government.

"Really always an agent for himself," Cleaves said. "Connie knew things about my work, very secret work for the government. I—I trusted her. She passed along things to Horween, and in the end Horween rigged a case against me. By then, not dreaming of what was going on, I had hired him as my executive assistant. Horween traded off information to a man named Lu-Feng, ostensibly head of a trade commission, actually a secret agent for the Red Chinese. It was made to look as if I had sold out. There were documents forged, tapes of conversations that could have double meanings. I was done for if I didn't do what Lu-Feng and Horween told me to do. I went along with it, hoping to find a way out, a way to get them."

During that time he stumbled on the truth about Horween and his wife. He went a little crazy. He started chasing available women all over London. He tried to humiliate Connie by taking them home to their house. She wasn't humiliated. She just laughed at him.

There was nothing to the story that Cleaves had something on Buck Ames. But she told Buck that Cleaves had something, and Ames who, like most men, had something to hide, believed that Cleaves knew what it was.

All the while Horween and Lu-Feng were putting the screws on Cleaves. Into the middle of this came Colin Andrews. He had wind of some kind of a sell-out. The trail led to Cleaves, when the guilty person was actually Horween, Cleaves's right-hand man.

The deeper Andrews dug, the closer he was coming to the truth without knowing it.

"A few more turns of the wheel and Horween's goose might have been cooked," Cleaves told us. "Horween and Connie were involved in this mad kidnapping scheme to raise enough money to live as they chose. I suspect they couldn't get around Lu-Feng. They were going to have to share with him. But there would be nothing for anybody if Andrews wasn't stopped. Horween couldn't do the job. He couldn't leave the fifteenth floor. I think you will find that it was up to Lu-Feng."

"I'd better go have a talk with him," Hardy said.

"I advise delay," Chambrun said. "I think Mr. Brand should tackle him first."

"Homicide isn't my department," Brand said.

"But the ransom money is," Chambrun said. "I think you'll find it was delivered to Lu-Feng by the men who posed as your agents. They couldn't risk running around in those vests stuffed with money and in those attack helmets. Someone in authority might give them orders, stop them. So I think you'll find they delivered the money to Lu-Feng, discarded their costumes, and are probably having a drink in the Trapeze Bar, waiting for the excitement to die down. Mr. Lu will plan, I think, to stay on at the hotel for a few days, then check out with his luggage—containing the money."

"Let's go get it now."

"One more thing, Mr. Cleaves," Chambrun said. "You beat up your wife, held her for the good part of a day in your room. It's not clear why."

Cleaves drew a deep breath. "She came to me to tell me that if I didn't raise the ransom money she would expose my supposed treachery. She's something of an actress, as you've seen. I almost believed it was out of concern for the children. But to expose me, certain forged documents, certain doctored tapes, were needed. I believed, as you did, that Horween was dead, killed by Coriander. That meant Connie had the faked evidence somewhere. I was desperate to get it."

Chambrun nodded slowly. Brand and Hardy took off to locate Mr. Lu-Feng.

"I'd like to go to the children and Katherine Horn," he said. "They're all going to need me and I've got, somehow, to make them understand. I've got, somehow, to make up to Katherine for what she's been through."

The sultry Miss Horn, I thought, meant more to him than a casual sex episode.

Chambrun and Ruysdale and I were finally alone. I was still in a state of shock.

"You'd better deal with the press, Mark," Chambrun said. "Get them off our backs and out of our hair. We've got a hotel to run." He hesitated. "There will be other women, the kind who will make it easy to forget Mrs. Cleaves."

"I was being so noble," I said, half laughing. "I was trying to be so goddamned noble and heroic."

He smiled at me. "It was probably very good exercise for you," he said.

Return to the scene of the crime with Worldwide Mysteries

COLD TRAIL—Dell Shannon $3.50 ☐
Detective Luis Mendoza marks the rising heat in Los Angeles by
the crime and violence raging through the streets—a thug is shot
to death, the body of a woman is found and a mysterious string
of robberies continues—all without a clue.

ALL BOOKED UP—Terrie Curran $3.50 ☐
A professor and his wife find themselves up against a brilliant
criminal when rare books mysteriously disappear from the
Boston University library and members of the staff turn up dead!

NO HARM—Wendy Hornsby $3.50 ☐
A young woman's life becomes endangered after she inherits a
palatial estate. Several near-fatal accidents fuel her growing fear
as she searches through generations of buried secrets to find the
portrait of a family killer.

Total Amount	$ _____
Plus 75¢ Postage	_____.75
Payment enclosed	$ _____

Please send a check or money order payable to Worldwide Library Mysteries.

In the U.S.	In Canada
Worldwide Library Mysteries	Worldwide Library Mysteries
901 Fuhrmann Blvd.	P.O. Box 609
Box 1325	Fort Erie, Ontario
Buffalo, NY 14269-1325	L2A 5X3

Please Print
Name: _____

Address: _____

City: _____

State/Prov: _____

Zip/Postal Code: _____

WORLDWIDE LIBRARY

Worldwide Mysteries make murder—most intriguing!

MURDER-BY-THE-SEA—Layne Littlepage $3.50 ☐
Opening night for the Carmel Playhouse was a killer—especially
when the body of an actress washed ashore. A former Hollywood
starlet investigating the death finds herself amidst a strange cast
of characters and someone in a murderous mood!

CRY AT DUSK—Mignon Ballard $3.50 ☐
A woman comes face-to-face with her darkest nightmare when
she returns to her small hometown to investigate the death of
her cousin and learns the secret of not one murder but two!

SPIT IN THE OCEAN—Shelley Singer $3.50 ☐
Private Eye Jake Samson becomes entangled in a strange case
involving a theft from a sperm bank in California. When a body
surfaces and attempts are made on Samson's own life, it
becomes apparent that someone wants him off the
case . . . permanently!

Total Amount	$ _____
Plus 75¢ Postage	.75
Payment enclosed	$ _____

Please send a check or money order payable to Worldwide Library Mysteries.

In the U.S.	In Canada
Worldwide Library	Worldwide Library
Mysteries	Mysteries
901 Fuhrmann Blvd.	P.O. Box 609
Box 1325	Fort Erie, Ontario
Buffalo, NY 14269-1325	L2A 5X3

Please Print

Name: _____

Address: _____

City: _____

State/Prov: _____

Zip/Postal Code: _____

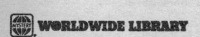

WØRLDWIDE LIBRARY

MYS-9

Winner of the Grand Master Award from the Mystery Writers of America, Dorothy Salisbury Davis "... has few equals in setting up a puzzle, complete with misdirection and surprises."
—*New York Times Book Review*

Julie Hayes Mysteries

LULLABY OF MURDER $3.50   ☐
When an infamous New York gossip columnist is found
murdered, reporter Julie Hayes starts digging and discovers a lot
of people are happier with him dead! As murder takes center
stage, Julie finds herself caught in a web of hate, deceit and
revenge, dirty deals and small-town scandals.

THE HABIT OF FEAR $3.50   ☐
New York columnist Julie Hayes struggles to regain her
equilibrium by traveling to Ireland in search of her father after a
seemingly random act of violence shatters her life. Her pursuit
leads her into a maze of violence, mystery—and murder.

Total Amount	$ _____
Plus 75¢ Postage	.75
Payment enclosed	$ _____

 **WORLDWIDE LIBRARY**